Three Hairy Women
by
Juana Walker

THREE HAIRY WOMEN

These stories are absolutely true, in the strict sense that everything recounted herein actually happened, and continues to happen. When these things happen, the names of the characters vary, of course, along with plot components and details.

Juana Walker

THREE
HAIRY
WOMEN

Erotic stories by

JUANA WALKER

Three Hairy Women

THREE HAIRY WOMEN

TABLE OF CONTENTS

Three Hairy Women

I: INCIDENT AND ANALYSIS

Jessica

I don't know why I'm suddenly able to do this. I do know why I haven't been able to do it before now: because I was afraid he wouldn't like it. I was afraid it might end our friendship, and I wouldn't be able to take it.

And now, I still know he may not like it, and I'll still be upset if he doesn't. But I'm not afraid, any more, that it may actually end our friendship. I believe, now, that we've become *best* friends, and that he would be as unwilling to give that up as I would.

Besides, I've planned it so that I can stop it if he responds poorly. Before the point of no return, that is. I'll have to watch his reactions very carefully. Surely, after three years, I know him well enough to read him right.

I'm still fighting my doubts, of course. I look around as I click along the sidewalk from my cubicle to his office. The familiar sights, all the memories. The feelings. The excitement when I first took this walk, the disbelief that he'd really invited me to "drop by" after work. And later, the comfortable weekly routine. I know I wouldn't want to lose that.

And of course, he has Mildred. Snooty bitch.

Still. The time has come. How can I lose him when I never really had him? Not the way I always wanted to have him. All we've ever been is buddies. And I always wanted more. Not just intimacy—in fact, I feel we've been intimate enough, although never physically, of course. He's always been fatherly toward me, or maybe older-brotherly. That's to be expected, I guess—he's ten years older than me, after all—but he still treats me, now, as he did when we first met. Back when I was starting my first job. He'd just got the promotion that marked him as headed toward top management. He knew the ropes, and I appreciated his willingness to explain them to me.

But he's still doing it. It's not that I don't still appreciate his advice. It's just that I need more equality in the mix. I'm tired of his assumption that I'm still a beginner. It makes me work too hard not to *feel* like a beginner.

But there's more to it than that. I'm tired of being . . . of being *dominated.* Even though his domination is very gentle and natural, and entirely intellectual. And emotional, too, I suppose. I just want him to see me as something more than a needy and worshipful little sister, even though I brought it on myself by playing that role too enthusiastically. It was I who scurried over to his office that next afternoon after the cocktail party. All starry-eyed.

The main thing I don't understand about him is why he can't see through Mildred! She obviously wants him just for his position and the impression he makes on her friends. She wants a trophy husband. Besides, she's so skinny he's in danger of getting stabbed in his sleep by one of her elbows.

8

She's right, I suppose, that he *is* good looking. Even though he's no hunk. He's not the muscular, deep-voiced suave type most young women go for. He's got nice shoulders, but he's kind of angular, and he has a high-cheekboned airiness about him that would make him too delicate if it weren't for his openness and self-confidence. Most women, including me, would rate him about eight, having taken a few minutes to notice him—which some women may not have done until called upon to rate him.

As for me, I'm maybe a seven. Maybe six. My features are a little heavy for beauty. My glasses are too thick—and I know that's the standard disqualification, but I tried contacts, and they were too uncomfortable. Or maybe I just couldn't be bothered. I'm not fat, but I'm no wispy angel. And fat is never far off. But I train regularly and watch my food and drink. While my hips are wide, my waist is relatively slim. I'm sure that if I were a man, I'd be even taller than he is, and more muscular. At least my brother is.

To be honest, I don't know why his good looks bother me.

But I do know that the time has come to do something about it. As I go through the revolving door and click-click across the marble foyer, I check myself out in the column mirror, as I always do. Everything's ready. It's casual Friday, and I'm in my low-cut jeans that I've never before dared wear outside my apartment. I've got a blouse on that looks like a man's white shirt, square-cut at the bottom, and which hangs far enough over the top of my jeans that my tummy doesn't show. As long as I keep my shoulders down.

Only my high heels, there to make me taller, are a little out of place
with my outfit.

Jill, his secretary, comes out of the elevator as I go in, and we
speak. Good—I won't have to wait to have him to myself.

As I ride up to his floor, a flash of fear rises from wherever I
suppressed it. Maybe he'll be disgusted. But I remind myself that
if he is, I don't want him anyway. I *don't*.

Brad

When Jessie showed up for our ritual Friday get-together, I
was on the phone with Ted. He was giving me trouble again. I had
a ritual going with him, too: I paid no attention to what he said, and
told him the kinds of things I always tell him. "I know, I know," I
was saying. "Do you think I like five o'clock Friday meetings? It
just has to be done before eight Monday morning. I told you that,
last Tuesday, and said for you to find a time. But I didn't hear from
you, so this is the price we both pay.

"Hi Jessie. Come on in." Dammit, if Ted didn't sell so much
product, I wouldn't have to put up . . .

"Of course, Ted, I know very well how busy you've been.
Me too. But this just has to be done. Would you prefer to come in
on Sunday? No, me neither. Look, if we can agree on the details, it
shouldn't take long, maybe thirty, forty minutes . . . OK? Right, in
the boardroom, so we can spread the stuff out. . . . For sure, we'll
have it to ourselves at five on a Friday. Right, in an hour. See
you."

"No, really?" said Jessie. "You have a meeting?" She'd stepped into the office, but was still hovering over by the door.

"Afraid so," I said, stretching. "But not for another hour. Come on in, get off your feet. We have time for a drink and our weekly catch-up. In fact, I need it." I rolled back in my chair and reached into the credenza for the Black Label and a couple of glasses. "I'd happily lose every meeting of the week, if I could, except this one."

"I hope that's true," she said. She closed the door and walked over to my desk, but didn't sit down. She looked oddly stiff—not her usual overcasual Friday self.

"So, what's up? Do you have to leave so soon? Go on, have a seat."

But she just stood there, gazing at me. Finally she said, "I'd rather stand. Been sitting all day."

Odd. "Suit yourself," I said, splashing the water into her scotch and setting it on the other side of the desk. "So, what's the latest over at Chaos Inc?"

"Oh, I don't know. Same as last week." That was even odder. She was normally brimming with office gossip. But then she smiled her usual relaxed smile, looking like Jessie for the first time since she came in, and took a sip of her whiskey.

Then she put down her glass, and to my surprise, walked around the desk. She stopped at the window and felt around behind the curtain, until she found the blind closer. She closed it. "Too bright in here," she said.

And then, she turned toward me, and after a short pause, did a big, luxuriant stretch.

I swear that my first reaction to what I saw was merely surprise. I caught only a quick glimpse of her tummy, and wasn't sure what I'd seen, and maybe stared a little too long. It was merely unexpected, and I was merely curious.

But then I realized that she was watching me the whole time, and that she'd seen me notice. When she finished her stretch, she was still looking at me with a little half-smile that I'd never seen on her face before. I was looking back at her, transfixed, and probably with my mouth open as well. At her face. I was scared to look anywhere else. I felt that I'd been caught staring at something I wasn't supposed to, like maybe a cripple, or a twelve-year-old girl with big tits, or my friend's dick. She had caught me in an indiscretion, and it was too late to do something ordinary and casual to give the impression that I hadn't noticed anything. She knew. So I stared, fixated, at her face, her little half-smile, completely at a loss about what to say or do next.

But I didn't have to worry long, because she did the next thing—and it was as surprising as the first few things. She walked over to my chair, with a kind of saunter, and put her hand on my shoulder. Behind my neck, resting lightly on my shoulder.

And why was it surprising? Because neither of us had ever done anything like that to each other before. I had been very careful, aside from kidding, to keep our friendship "platonic," as they say. I'd never touched her, except for the ritual hello or goodbye hug—the kind of hug that clearly says, "Not too long. Not too close. That's enough."

But what she was doing wasn't that kind of touch at all. She was standing so close I was enveloped by her perfume. It occurred to me how easy it would be to lift her shirt, just to see if what I'd seen was really there. And why not? We were friends. Quite old friends. Maybe I was being invited to look. If she wanted to show me something, why shouldn't I look at it?

And yet, I also knew she might misinterpret my curiosity. Did I really want that? What about Mildred? I'd never been actually physically attracted to Jessie. Now's the time, I thought, to stop this in its tracks. Just stand up and give her a platonic hug, and go to my meeting early.

But first, I lifted her shirt.

And there it was. It could have been some weird sort of garment I'd seen, but it wasn't. It was a wide growth of dark hair. It arose from under her jeans, fluffing over the top edge, and covered her navel, and continued upwards, diminishing, until what remained disappeared under her raised shirt.

I was simply amazed. Women aren't this hairy. It struck me that she was hairier down there than I am.

And I was right that she would see my move as more than an attempt to satisfy my curiosity. While I stared, she gave my shoulder a little squeeze with the hand that was there, and with the other hand she held up the bottom of her shirt, relieving me of that chore.

"Feel it," she said.

I suppressed my impulse to say, "Feel what?" But that left me with *nothing* to say.

So I felt it. I wrapped my nearest arm around her hips, and with my other palm and fingers, I felt her hair. It was fine and soft and thick. I guess I sort of petted it, for quite a long time.

This was very strange. I was acting and responding according to *her* interpretation of what was going on rather than mine. I don't know where she got the idea that her hairy tummy was attractive—so attractive that I would want to pet it. I would never have thought so. But that's what I was doing.

Maybe I didn't want to hurt her feelings. Her assurance that she was giving me something special was touching. I didn't want to ruin it for her.

I've heard being hypnotized is like that. You know you can break out of it any time. Just say, "OK, that's enough." It would be so easy to do, however, that you don't feel it's really necessary. Besides, you don't want to disappoint the hypnotist. So you just pretend you're under the spell.

As I was trying to figure it all out, she made her next move. I was holding her hip against me anyway, so all she had to do was bend me over a little and twist my head sideways, and her tummy was in my face. The perfume was obviously in the hair, stronger but still subtle. Her hands were now on both sides of my head. She didn't press; she just sort of guided my face around while I kissed and nuzzled. Her tummy was very warm.

We did that for quite a long time too. I was in a bit of an awkward position, bent over in my chair with my neck twisted. So finally, I slipped out of my chair, onto my knees. That was better.

But my shift had another unexpected effect. She moved back a step and unbuttoned her shirt. I noticed that her glasses had disappeared, and so had her half-smile. In their place was an intense brown-eyed gaze. She unbuttoned her jeans, hooked both thumbs over them and her panties, pulled them down all the way to the carpet, and stepped out of them, as well as her high heels. Then she reached down and put her shoes back on. As she stood up, my eyes were once again fixed on her face; but she looked down at herself, so I looked too.

Her strip of tummy hair widened and became her pubic hair, which was itself so wide that I was stunned all over again. Immediately she stepped forward. Her hand returned to its place behind my head, and she buried my face in her warm, fragrant, extravagant hairiness.

At that point things became really confusing. One reason they were confusing was that they shouldn't have been. For the first time in the whole encounter, I was in familiar territory. I often go down on my girlfriends (one at a time, I should mention), usually as a preamble to getting them to go down on me. But that was one of the confusing things—in the past, it had always been my preamble, my plan. I'd had nothing to do with *this* plan. I hadn't even been consulted.

Another thing was that, until now, I'd been able to think that Jessie was just revealing her secret to her closest male friend, maybe to solicit my approval and enable her to feel better about herself. Of course, I had to go along with that. But what was happening now was different. This was sex.

I ought just to stop it, right now, I thought again.

While I was thinking about that, I sort of automatically started licking her. I probed my tongue through her mat, and felt around, guided by my trained instincts, but also by her helping hand and an adjustment in the presentation of her torso. I felt until I found her clit. What followed was just a matter of habit, although I soon became more lost in it than usual—more than ever before, in fact.

The astonishing absurdity of my position did occur to me at some point. Here I was, *on the floor,* behind my desk in *my own office,* being *fucked in the face* by *Jessie,* who, scarcely thirty minutes before, was still the innocent young girl I'd benevolently taken on as a sort of apprentice because she clearly adored me and didn't have a lot going for her. And most absurd of all, I'd had nothing to do with this ridiculously sudden and possibly catastrophic shift in my understanding of the way things are between us.

But the rest of the time, as I say, I was just lost. Jessie was making a small slow movement with her hips, rocking my head gently back and forth, but my tongue was doing most of the work. Her fingers were gripping my shoulder, now, to stabilize the wobble of her stilettos, and her other fingers were pressing the back of my head.

I felt her movements getting a little faster; and then I was brought out of my daze by the little vibration between her legs that told me I could stop—a tiny shudder that would become very familiar during our subsequent encounters. Only one of my previous girlfriends climaxed in that particular way, and it certainly wasn't Mildred who, as far as I could tell, never climaxed at all, although she pulled off some pretty spectacular fakes.

I took my hands off Jessie's hips. She stepped back and scooped up her panties. *My* clothes were all still on. I hadn't even unzipped my trousers. In fact, it occurred to me, I'd never even kissed Jessie—in the customary places, that is.

"You better wash your face before your meeting," she said. Her old full smile was back. She put her jeans on, and leaving her shoes, she walked around the desk, grabbing her scotch on the way, and went on around and sat in my chair. She put on her glasses, and touched my mouse to bring my computer to life.

"Aren't you leaving?" I asked, as I got up off my knees.

"No, I'll wait for you." she said. "I'm not finished with you yet."

Analysis: Brad

It took me a long time to figure out what happened to me that late afternoon, and why I liked it enough to accept the change in our relationship that Jessie imposed on me so unmistakably. And, to break things off with Mildred, just to be fair to both of them.

They say that some predatory fish stun their prey by thwacking them first, to make them easier to catch and eat. That's what Jessie did to me. Before I could recover, the banquet had begun.

She did it in a strange way. It had to be strange to be unexpected; if I had expected it, I would have defended myself against it. For a few moments—maybe an hour, who knows—she stole away an essential component of who I am, and so enabled me, for that same length of time, to lose myself. The component she took away was one I could never have chosen to give up, not even for an hour.

She usurped my masculinity.

She did it by being more masculine than I was, in a way that I could accept as entirely non-threatening. Maybe only Jessie could have done that for me, since I knew *she* was non-threatening (although for a while, there, I didn't know *what* she was).

You have to understand, if you don't already, that a male executive's sense of masculinity is bound up with his feeling of control. I suppose the same may be true of a female executive. Yes, I mean that her sense of masculinity—of *her* masculinity, as urged by the often high levels of testosterone that inform her personality— is tied together with her assurance that she can control the people and situations she supervises. All executives must exercise control all day, all week, on and on, for the rest of their careers.

And if they're any good, they find it impossible to give up control. I'm not talking about ordinary evening relaxation. Lounging with your feet up, you may not be controlling things for the time being, but your *sense* of control—your knowing who and what you are—never leaves you, as long as you're awake. The only way it could leave you would be for you somehow to lose your *self.*

But just at the time I was letting my guard down, anticipating only a pleasant short break from that long hard day, Jessie began to take over—with such innocent stealth that I didn't recognize it as a takeover. By the time I figured it out I was enjoying it too much to care.

She used her hairiness to surprise and confuse me; but then that same feature played into the next move in her strategy. It was a while afterward before I recognized that I still think of body hair as a masculine symbol. I thought I'd left that behind with my other teenage broodings about masculinity, along with dick measurements and obnoxious assertiveness, in favor of trained intelligence, careful grooming, confident professionalism, skill in negotiations—that sort of thing. But she, just by assuming that *her* hair was sexy, in a context in which it would have been rude to disagree, and by insisting that it be the focus of our encounter—she sneaked it by me.

And then she *used* me to satisfy herself—and then she abandoned me. Temporarily. Any woman will tell you that's a very manly thing to do. Or at least a male thing. What I don't get is why they don't *like* being used. I certainly did, once I got over my confusion. Still do.

19

And the reason it's satisfying is that it's such a relief to momentarily lose the responsibility for being manly—to let a natural master driver take the reins, and to just enjoy the ride. She assured me later that it only worked because I was confident enough in my manliness to let it go. I accept that.

And, as I said, you can't lose such a key dimension of your self and keep your self. A lot is made these days, in some circles, about finding yourself. I'd say losing yourself takes the prize any day.

As for Jessie, I'm full of admiration for her courage. If she really values our friendship as much as she says, she took a hell of a chance.

Analysis: Jessica

The trouble with Frank is that he's too insensitive to get it. Besides, he's so hairy himself he probably won't be impressed with me. Still, it's worth a try.

At first, I was relieved at how easy Brad was. I needed that assurance about myself. And I don't want to give him up. I feel very close and comfortable with him. But he's just . . . I don't know. He's become nothing *but* easy. I still find him attractive, but he just collapses whenever I approach him sexually. He's like putty in my hands. It's almost as if he's not in there—not the Brad I know. Knew. Besides, he doesn't feel my butt and thighs nearly enough while he's licking me.

Frank won't be as easy. Maybe he won't respond at all, or maybe he'll even make fun of me. But I know he's interested. Of course, he doesn't really know me yet. But it's worth a try.

II: THE CON

Thinking back on it, I suppose the young lady was right—I must have been staring. The big cheap Italian cafe at the mall was full for lunchtime, and I guess I assumed I was lost in the crowd. It didn't occur to me that the little teenage girl (thirteen or fourteen, I guessed) would have noticed me looking at her, much less that she would have confronted me about it.

The only thing about her that interested me, at first, was her eyebrow. Right, only one eyebrow. It did a double William and Mary-style arch over her eyes, and true to the style was connected in the middle, with no sign of any plucking or any other kind of weeding out. And it was its unplucked state that interested me most, because, I suppose, of what it said about the brain dwelling behind it. A bold brain. Standing above, and in total contempt for, the fears and fashions that usually beset girls her age.

And what happened then, after my curiosity had been excited, convinced me that what I was looking at was something even more impressive than boldness. It was confidence. Even independence.

She stared back.

I immediately looked away, of course. I looked down at my plate, and decided I'd better eat the remaining piece of caneloni I'd earlier decided to leave. Then I looked at some of the silly Italian things hanging on the walls. But when I looked back her way, having given her all the time she needed to return to her adolescent preoccupations, she was still staring at me.

I smiled at her, but her expression didn't change.

And then, she got up, and walked toward my table. I looked away again, and didn't look back until she was standing there and couldn't be ignored.

"I'm way too young for you," she said.

"I know. I know," I responded. "I wasn't . . . I wasn't thinking of anything like that, at all. I was just . . ."

"And what's a lot worse, you're way too old for me."

I couldn't think of a quick comeback for that, which was a good thing, because it gave me a chance to catch myself. Why was I feeling defensive, with this little teenager? The main thing I wanted to do, now that she was standing there, was escape without hurting her feelings. She was probably really quite sensitive about her brow . . . although on the other hand . . .

"Then why were you staring at me?" she demanded.

"Well. You *are* quite an attractive young lady," I managed.

Then she did smile, but not the smile of flattered pleasure. A sort of cynical half-smile. And she remained standing there in front of my table, looking me over. I seem to remember she had her arms firmly crossed in front of her. I also remember being relieved that the table was between us, in case my fly was open. I couldn't think of any other reason for her scrutiny, although it couldn't have been that. Because of the table, see. Then it occurred to me that she was giving me the opening I needed for a retaliation.

"And why are you staring at *me*?" I said.

"Give me your number," she responded, throwing a pen on the table. I guess she must have brought the pen off *her* table. I'd seen the waitress lady leave the bill a minute earlier. And I vaguely remembered that somebody else had been there, as well. None of it was clear.

"Hurry. On that paper. That napkin. Here she comes."

It was Mama, I guessed. She arrived back at their table, and was sorting cash from her purse and putting it in the little plastic folder thing, but all the time giving us hard glances. Not friendly glances. It seemed to run in the family.

Well why not give her a number? What harm could it do? Maybe the little girl needed someone to talk to. So, I wrote my number on the napkin. Not my phone number. My e-mail address. I don't tweet. My new friend grabbed the napkin and stuffed it in her jeans pocket, just before Mama marched over and seized her by the arm.

"Frieda, I told you not to do that. Come on."

Frieda! Really! She had named her little girl after the most famous single-brow woman in history! How had she known what her baby's brows would look like?

I now found myself staring at the mother. She had two brows, in the common arrangement, one over each eye. But the arches were the same shape as her daughter's, and I was staring at the space between them to see if I could detect signs of plucking.

"I'm sorry," Mama said to me. "Ignore her, please. It's a bad habit she has." And she hauled her off. As she was being pulled toward the door, the daughter looked back and smiled at me again, but this time, I was pretty sure, it was a real smile. A friendly smile, or close.

Mama let go after just a few steps, and the two of them proceeded out into the mall. They were small dark energetic creatures, with blazing dark eyes, and dark brown hair tied back into long pony tails. Mare's tales. They both had jeans on, and for the first time I noticed, as they walked away, that they were both quite shapely, with lithe long waists and nice wide teardrop butts, of the kind I like—as do all men, probably. Mama's was bigger, and her jeans were kind of baggy. But Frieda, I decided, was a little older than I'd thought originally.

Nothing came of the encounter right away. And of course, I didn't care. She really was too young for me, and I congratulated myself on giving her only my first name and e-mail rather than my telephone number, while wondering why I'd gone even that far.

And yet I found myself thinking about them. What an odd pair they were. And why, if, as she'd said, she was not only too young for me, but I was also too old for her—why, then, had she asked for my "number"? What did that mean? And where did people like that come from? Gypsies? A family of con artists? And if so, what was their game? Of course, my main instinct was wariness, and gratitude that they were leaving me alone.

And yet, curiosity—which, as we all know, continues to kill cats—had me guessing and speculating about who and what they were, and even rehearsing dialogues designed to get information from them while giving nothing away that they could use to con me.

But in spite of the fact that my mind continued to return to that incident, and my imagination to dwell on it, I was surprised when the e-mail came a couple of days later. But most of all, pleased and relieved. A part of me was thinking, "Oh, no," and deciding to ignore it. But the part of me that had been disappointed, because I hadn't heard, was delighted, and beginning to plan a strategy for self-protection as I ventured back into dangerous territory.

The e-mail said: "Paul—Bistro Whatever again, next Friday at noon. Italian place in the mall. You pay for lunch. Reply. I'm not coming unless you'll be there.—Frieda."

I was working in my studio, although I didn't have any appointments that day. I found myself walking aimlessly and excitedly around the room for a minute. And then I got my workout bag out of the closet. Apparently I was going to the gym. I hadn't planned to go, and in fact hadn't gone there for weeks. Whatever my reason for going now, I told myself I needn't question it. I'd been trying to make myself get back into my workouts, and now I was doing it.

But I was aware that it had something to do with my stupid excitement, which had something to do with the message from Frieda; and warning bells were ringing in my head, and the paranoid voice was back, telling me I had to be very careful. She was almost certainly underage. I knew that, and reminded myself of the roles I could play, and in fact had been practicing. Suave but assertive older . . . but no. Big brother? Well, not really. It wouldn't get me where I wanted to go, wherever that was. Concerned uncle? I would be "avuncular." What a word. It's innocent—it just means "like an uncle"—but it sounds much worse.

I kept thinking about all of this, all the time looking in the mirror, while I was doing my weight training. I work out for my health, of course. I cycle when weather permits, and if it doesn't permit for a while, I get on the exercise cycle at the gym. And also weights. I'm proud of my almost-young-looking body, and would like to keep it looking almost young as long as I can, of course. But that means vanity, and not just health, also plays a role in motivating me to persist in the exercise. So, why not? I told myself again. Any motivation that gets me into the gym can't be bad.

But why now? Suddenly, after weeks of lethargy? And what was the reason for my continued high feeling, as I worked my way through my weights routine?

I made myself face it. It was that little girl, of course. The attention she was giving me, whatever her reason, in the midst of what had turned into a long and lonely phase of my life. Maybe, I'd even realized, a permanent phase.

There was something about her forthrightness, her independence, and . . . and yes, her long slim waist expanding

downwards and outwards into a surprising width where her

28

thighs continued the contour. And all, somehow—this is the strange part—all an expression of, and dominated by, that eyebrow.

And my suspicion that I had mis-estimated her age. My hope.

Maybe she's eighteen. Maybe she goes for older guys, and her talk about my being too old for her was just an attempt to talk herself out of her "bad habit," as her mother called it. But now, she was yielding to the pressure.

What a pathetic creature I am. And what a target for a con!

All the same, I continued my workout. And my high, for the rest of the day. And when I got back to my studio, I answered Frieda's e-mail. Sure, I often have lunch there. I can be there Tuesday, if you want to talk to me.

Why not?

And I was there, half-an-hour before twelve. It wouldn't do for her to show up first, maybe decide I wasn't coming. She might leave.

I decided to pass the time with a glass of chianti, even though I never drink at lunch. It would help me relax. I cleared my mind of plots and plans and opening lines. She'd called the meeting, after all. As long as I could avoid being nervous, I could be pretty good at small talk. Let her take the lead, state her purpose. I would be cool. That's what teenagers go for, right? Congenial but cool.

I knew, of course, that I did have to prepare my frame of mind. I couldn't let that take care of itself, because what might come out if I did might be the real pathetic me. That obviously wouldn't do. I had to "get into the character," as the method actors say. Practice my avuncularism. Kindly trustworthy uncle. And trusting, too, or apparently so. I hadn't really decided to go with that, since it wasn't the way I really wanted to present myself, but that was the last one I'd thought of, and I needed something. I had to go with the facts, not the fantasies. Until the fantasies became facts. Unlikely, I reminded myself again.

But the difficult part was that I couldn't really be trusting. I had to be suspicious and alert, ready to see the con clearly, when it appeared, or at least sniff any foul smells that came floating by. That is, I had to be two opposite things, neither of which was the real me. Even the method actors would have trouble with that. Appearing to be open and honest while at the same time nearly covering up a street-smart analytical side. Actors who could pull that off were considered geniuses. Of course, I did something like that with new clients, all the time. But that was the difference. All clients are pretty much alike. But Frieda was different.

What had I got myself into?

I realized, with a jolt, that I had allowed myself to slump into a posture of defeat, before I'd even begun the contest. And more— without being aware of it, I'd let an instinctive urge develop within me, that was just about to take over and make me do something. I pushed back my chair, and stood up. What was I going to do?

Then I knew, to my distress, that I was about to walk out! Give up the whole thing, on impulse, without a further thought!

And indeed, why shouldn't I? Well, because I'd said I'd be here, that's why I shouldn't. But an emergency had come up, hadn't it? I'd just figured out that I'd got myself into an impossible situation. My desires had overwhelmed my understanding, and like a fool—a much younger fool—I had chosen to side with my desires.

But getting out now would work. She'd show up—or maybe not, who knows? But if she did, she'd wait maybe fifteen minutes, then she'd be gone, having suffered no real harm, and I'd never see her again. Maybe a nasty e-mail that I could easily ignore . . .

But now I see she has already shown up. She's at the door, looking around. Now she's seen me. I'm standing, after all. Her face breaks into a smile—a real one. She says something to the girl behind the hostess stand, and starts weaving her way across to my table, her wide hips swaying past the chairs, and that eyebrow dominating the whole room. I feel that all the diners have suddenly become silent, and are watching her in wonder at her strangeness, and at her strange and unaccountable splendor, as she advances toward me.

I start to sit down, defeated. Then I realize she must think I stood to greet her, so I remain standing, forcing a clumsy smile of my own. As she gets closer I see she's wearing a skirt; and as she glances down to edge sideways between two chair backs, I glance down too, to see her legs. They're obscured by shadow, but I can see that they're slim but with nicely full calves. And as she

31

turns sideways, I can't miss the contour of her butt. And now she's here, still smiling.

"Hello, Paul," she says.

"Hello, Frieda. Have a . . ." But she's already having a seat, in the chair opposite mine, so I sit too. Now I can hear the noise of the crowd of diners again, as though it had never stopped.

She took a deep breath, almost a sigh, and just sat for a moment and smiled at me. For that moment I thought that my plan to let her take the lead wasn't going to work, and I began to panic, trying to think of something to say. I didn't want to rush into the business at hand, whatever that was, because I wasn't ready to think yet. Then, just in time, she said, "Have you ordered?" Looking at my empty wine glass.

"No. Waiting for you."

She took the lunch menu from the rack at the edge of the table and started looking through it, so I did the same. But I knew what I wanted, so I watched her as she scanned the menu. I noticed that sitting, she was nearly as tall as I was. That would be her long waist. I was feeling small.

She replaced the menu, and announced, "I'll have the tilapia. And ice tea."

"So will I," I said. "That's easy." That wasn't what I'd decided before, but it really was easier. She seemed to expect me to order for her, and I was afraid I'd get forgetful if I tried to remember two different orders, in my present nervous condition.

But when the waiter arrived immediately, taking me by surprise, she said, "We're both having the lunch tilapia. And I'll have iced tea."

"Two tilapias," said the waiter. "And another chianti for you, Sir?"

"Uh . . . well, yes. Why not?" I added a chuckle. But, of course, that wasn't what I'd decided before either.

This was really bizarre. My attempt at method acting had only gone halfway. I'd managed to cease to be the person I was—a person who knew what he wanted for lunch—but I hadn't yet become the person my assigned role called for. Or had I? I was doing a pretty good imitation of a chuckling uncle. What I was, really, was confused. And the result was, I was about to eat a lunch I didn't really want. And drink too much wine.

Could this little girl be a witch?

She just sat there, putting her big paper napkin in her lap. When she saw me looking at her, she smiled again, ignoring, I guess, that I was staring at her in horror. Maybe I wasn't. Who knows? Her dark eyes, which had been flashing last time I saw her, were sparkling now. Under that looming brow.

I still needed to think of something to say. What came out was, "How did you get here?"

"Get here?" She looked slightly puzzled. "Oh, you mean to the mall. I drove. Ann's car. Ann's my mother. You met her. Or almost."

"So, you drive?"

"When I need to." Her answer had the tone of, Yes, of course, didn't I just say so? "And when I can borrow a car," she continued. "And how did you get here?"

"I walked. I'm only around the corner."

"Do you have a car?"

"Not now. I manage with rail and taxi. And airplane, but rarely, these days. I used to need a car, when I had to go see lots of clients. Now I work mainly from blueprints and snapshots. I can do most of it by e-mail or courier. When we need to meet, they mostly come to me."

"Blueprints. So, you're a . . . you're a . . ."

"Sort of a specialty designer. Interiors. My training is in architecture." It felt good to talk about myself. It reminded me of who I was. "And what do you do?"

"I'm in school, of course. When I'm not on break."

School. College? And then it just came out, before I knew what I was saying. "How old are you?" I asked. I wasn't anywhere near ready for her answer, whatever it was. But it was done—the question was out there.

"How old are *you*?" she retorted. That was a relief. It put me in more familiar territory. People my age play that game all the time. I'll tell you if you tell me. Then when you tell each other, it's like you're confessing deep secrets. It's a ritual of getting closer. Icebreaking.

"I'll have to think about that one," I said, chuckling some more. "I've lost count. Anyway, you've already told me I'm too old for you."

But then she said, "I'm sixteen."

Sixteen. She said sixteen.

Well, what had I expected? I had hoped for eighteen, of course. Maybe even older. True, if she'd said eighteen, I wouldn't have believed her. Well, I would have believed her for a while, even if I had the strong suspicion she was lying. I guess that was the main con I'd put myself on guard against. She lies about her age, gets me entangled, then they take advantage of my guilt. Sort of blackmail me.

But to my dismay, I realized that I might have been hoping that I could go along with that plot. I wouldn't be the first guy to take care of his girl, and her old mother as well. I just hadn't seen it as yielding to a con.

But suddenly another, grimmer thought struck me. The illegality—the underage child. They wouldn't even need to blackmail me. They could report me, press charges, demonize me, sue me, disappear with my money while I was in prison!

The fact that I hadn't considered that little feature made it clear what a dream I'd been dreaming. Nobody is more vulnerable to a con than someone who wants to be conned. And nobody deserves it more. I'd actually been sort of planning my dream. Figuring out exactly how I'd handle things, and what I wanted from my very expensive arrangement, besides to stay out of jail. Although in fact I suspect I already knew what I wanted.

But sixteen. She was supposed to lie. She had no reason to say she was sixteen if it weren't true.

She was looking at me with concern. "Are you okay?" she asked. "You look a little . . . a little lost."

"Lost!" I chuckled again, this time ironically. "Yeah, I'd say that's the word for it. But I'm okay. Look, here's lunch." The server gave us our drinks. A girl showed up right behind him with our tilapias. I had a few good swallows of my chianti. Maybe I'd need another glass.

"Ann's a receptionist for a law firm," said Frieda, while our meals were being laid out. "I got her the job. She's been there a couple of years. She's a very friendly person."

"How did you get her the job?"

"Oh, I knew some of the lawyers. I know lots of people. I'm good at meeting people."

"I'd have to agree with that," I said, while suppressing a little twinge of jealousy that she knew young lawyers that well. And then it hit me—they had friends who were lawyers! No doubt one or two as besotted with her as I was! And she'd met them and besotted them when she was . . . what? Fourteen years old?

And with that, I backed off. Emotionally, that is. The whole scene was too much for me. And I didn't seem to be thinking terribly clearly.

After my emotional resignation, the lunch hour went a little better for me. We talked quite a lot—at least I did. It turned out she wasn't a big talker. She was a big questioner. I felt, at first, that I was being interviewed. But the interviewer was so sympathetic I soon opened up to her. Maybe it was nerves. Or maybe a reaction against my role-playing. But I answered all her questions, at length, without a trace of self-consciousness. I no longer had to play the chuckling uncle—I had *become* him.

I went ahead and had my third glass of chianti, but then stopped short of a fourth, to demonstrate my self-control. Someone refilled her tea, and she took the occasional sip.

I told her about how I chose the university I went to, something she was just starting to think about. I told her about the sad departure of my wife, all those years ago. How long it had taken me to get back on my feet. I didn't tell her I'd never quite got back on my feet. I told her how I'd found my career niche. Maybe it would help her find hers. Because she laughed with me whenever I chuckled, and immediately asked another question, showing every sign of interest, I thought we were communicating. Only later did I realize that I'd done all the talking. She'd told me nearly nothing about herself.

One thing I did find out about her, as we were eating. She had a long-sleeved blouse on, but manipulating her fish and reaching for her tea, her sleeves kept slipping up an inch or so, and I caught glimpses of the fine, dark hair on her arms. Fine but ample. Her eyebrow wasn't the only part of her body she didn't trim to fit the fashions.

We finished, and I paid. As we left the restaurant, to my surprise, she slipped her hand into my arm. To my greater surprise, she pulled herself close to me. I could feel her little breast pressed against my arm, and my fingers were touching her thigh. We stopped. "I enjoyed talking with you, Paul," she said. "And Paul . . . I like you a lot. And Ann said if I like you, I should invite you over for dinner. So . . . can you come next Friday evening? In a week. About eight?"

I was totally unprepared, and totally unnerved. "Well, sure. Sure, I can come. Sure. Thanks! I'll enjoy it."

"Good. And Paul . . . one other thing. Don't worry. Everything'll be okay. I promise." She gave my arm a little squeeze, and then she was walking away. "I'll e-mail you the address," she added, looking back and smiling again.

I watched her go, and embarrassed though I was that she felt she had to reassure me about "everything," I couldn't help but notice one more disquieting thing about her body. Her legs were very shapely, but they weren't hairy, as I expected. But then as she walked further, I could see some dark bands showing below the edge of the skirt, like the bottoms of some sort of long tight-fitting underpants. Then it struck me that she'd shaved below that point, but had left a little bit showing. Deliberately, no doubt.

She was too much. She was entirely too much for me. I couldn't have her, whatever her age.

38

But she wanted to be friends, and that made me happy. Stupidly and comically happy.

I managed to get through the next week relatively calmly, in spite of my sequence of mind changes—doubts followed by decisions to back out followed by failures to do so. I convinced myself that her invitation was just a friendly gesture, offered, probably, out of sympathy for the poor bumbling fool I'd turned into at the restaurant. And hadn't she said—promised—that everything would be all right? I believed her.

How pathetic.

When Friday evening finally came, I took a taxi over to the address she'd sent me. I'd been a little surprised about the part of town where they lived, a recently gentrified area full of old refurbished mansions—too upscale and costly for a receptionist, however big the law firm. I expected to find Frieda and her mother in a couple of rooms in one of the still-unrefurbished frame buildings, maybe in a basement. Not so. The address was one of the nicer four-story brownstones, nicely restored. And while it was divided into apartments, theirs was on the first floor up, the prime situation in the place. And I soon found out they had the whole floor.

As I waited for her to answer the doorbell, I couldn't ward off the return of my suspicions. This much money couldn't come from Ann's job, so it had to come from somewhere else. Inheritance, followed by careful investments? Okay. But if not, maybe someone else's money. If so, where was he? Maybe I was about to meet him. Or maybe it came from my predecessors in this business—poor besotted fools, now rotting away in some distant prison, while these two black widows feasted on . . .

She opened the door, and there she was, beaming at me. Warm air rushed out, enveloped me, filled with strong warm smells of Mediterranean cooking. I returned her smile, and walked into her lair. She immediately seized my arm again. Where we'd left off, I thought.

"To the kitchen," she said. "Time to meet Mama."

I decided, as we walked down the hall, her warm body once again pressed against my arm, that I would have to just ask her some questions. I no longer felt that I had to be all that careful about the impression I made, or about hiding my suspicions. She'd asked me plenty of questions at the restaurant. And I'd answered them all. Now it was her turn.

Mama was at the stove. She shoved a pot aside and wiped her hands on a towel. Her dark eyes were glowing. "Frieda tells me you like Italian," was her opening line. "I hope so, cause that's what it is. A little Spanish."

"Love it," I said. "Particularly northern." I could tell by the fish and garlic smells where the recipe came from. There was lots of cooking stuff on the counters, and a cutting board with different kinds of cheese on it, a bowl of grapes, half a glass of red wine. I predicted that this lady knew her food. "Are you Italian, perchance?"

"No, no. Good guess, though. I'm mostly Armenian. Frieda's more Armenian than I am." She turned and walked toward me, her hand extended, wearing a red apron and some sort of white cotton jacket above her slacks. She had pushed back the sleeves, and I could tell at a glance she also had her daughter's fine hair covering her arms. It was odd that my first thought was that she'd got it from her daughter, rather than the other way around. She had her daughters' smile, as well. And her daughter's eyebrow, I decided, with the middle mechanically or chemically deleted. We shook.

"This is Paul," said Frieda. "Paul, Ann."

"You're welcome, Paul," said Ann. "I also hope you like spicy. Most people do, these days."

"Of course," I said. I really do—but I wondered exactly how spicy Armenian is.

"Oh, good. I was a little worried. Make yourself at home, please. Frieda, keep him entertained. Get him some wine—I just opened some, in the front fridge. Put on some music. I'll have this ready in a few minutes."

In spite of Ann's ease with the formalities, I got the distinct impression that she was a little nervous.

Frieda, who was not nervous, sat me in the living room, where I immediately recognized the work of my friend Gustavo Zimmerman in the slight style update, including the ceiling treatment he'd lifted from me. We did that with each other—he in residential, I in commercial—although I disapproved of his doing it in this sort of building. Frieda handed me a glass of nice crisp wine that tasted like a decent California sauvignon blanc but was probably something Italian, I guessed; and she put on some equally cool saxaphone jazz that I didn't recognize. "Suit you?" she asked.

"Yes indeed," I said. "But suit yourself."

"Oh, no. That wouldn't suit you," she responded. That bothered me—more about our age difference, I guessed. But I let it pass. The domestic conventionality of the reception I was getting and, as far as I could tell, of the whole setup here, was making it hard to believe that there was anything to worry about—or anything, really, to look forward to, except maybe a good Italian meal. And maybe a new friendship or two. But I decided to ask a few questions to just get things lined up better.

"What did Ann mean, that you're more Armenian than she is?" I asked, to get my questions started.

"Oh, Ann's only half Armenian. Her mother was from there. But my dad was a hundred percent. So, I guess I'm three-quarters. I don't know why she makes so much of that. I mean, he was a hundred percent American, after he came here, right? And so am I, right?"

"Sure, right. You say your dad 'was.' Is he . . . is he still around?"

"We don't know where he is," said Frieda, a little off-handed.

42

I knew not to keep on with that, but I couldn't resist one more question. "Do you ever see him?"

"I only met him once," she said. "I liked him. He's a good man."

Hmm. Well, that was something, but I still hadn't pinned it down. I couldn't think of how to ask my next question, so we just listened to the music for a while. A Hawkins imitator, or the man himself, although I didn't know the recording. If an imitator, a very good one. And the cornetist and pianist were top-notch too.

After pondering for a while, I decided to start the next conversation. "This is a very nice place," I commented. "Do you rent?"

"No, it's ours," said Frieda. "Just this floor, the condo. Ann bought it three . . . four years ago."

"But it belongs to Frieda," said Ann, as she entered the room. "Could you help me get stuff on the table, Baby? Dinner's served, Paul, if you'd like to come. We can hear the music in there."

I shuffled in there, behind the ladies, wondering how I could get an explanation for this last little revelation. But by the time I got into the dining room and sat down, there was something else on my mind.

It was Ann. A transformation had come over her. She'd removed her apron and jacket thing, leaving a black sort of sleeveless blouse or knit thing that was tight around her neck but revealed her arms and shoulders. I'd only glanced at her in the living room; and as she walked ahead of me down the hall and turned into the kitchen, I'd caught a glimpse of the shape of her butt, which I'd been looking forward to glimpsing. And something else. Something else, quite unexpected.

I stared straight ahead at a sideboard against the opposite wall, not daring to look anywhere else, while Ann served little plates with jiggling cubes of jelled gazpacho on lettuce, and Frieda poured the rest of the white wine out of a half-empty bottle. I was afraid to look at Ann to confirm what I'd seen—afraid I'd be unable to stop looking and make a fool of myself staring at her.

Instead I looked at Frieda, as she settled into her chair, and was disturbed to find her staring at *me*, almost expectantly. I was confused again. I decided she wanted a reaction to the first course— Ann was seated now, too, and they both seemed to be waiting for me to get started—so I took a little taste of the gazpacho. "Umm," I said. "Tasty." Then I lifted my wine glass and said, "To new friendships."

That seemed to please them. "New friendships," they both said, and we all sipped our wine.

I looked over at Ann—it seemed a natural thing to do, now—and glanced down slightly, and very quickly, enough to confirm what I thought I'd seen earlier. I realized immediately, to my consternation, that she'd seen me look, and knew what I was looking at. I turned my attention to Frieda, as if I were just checking out my new friends; but the half smile on her face told me that she'd also seen me look at her mother. So I looked back at the safe sideboard, and took another sip of my wine. More of a swallow.

It was her breasts. Ann's breasts. In all the other important ways she looked like her daughter, so I expected her breasts to be smallish. But they were full and rounded, and very natural looking, bundled in their black bag, as though unsupported by any other paraphernalia. On a bigger woman they may not have been anything special. But Ann was small, and they occupied her whole chest.

I got into the gazpacho, which was tasty as I said, and refreshing as it should be. And Ann, possibly now that I'd made the ritual gestures Armenians require to get an evening started— including acknowledging the size of the hostess's chest—Ann became quite talkative. As it turned out, I didn't have to probe to get the explanations that had been my primary concern only a few minutes earlier.

"You were asking about this condo," she said. "I bought it with money from the fund Azad set up for Frieda. Azad was—is— Frieda's father, and I first met him at the Armenian club in Philly. I used to go there with my parents. Actually, it was the Armenian *night* at the Baltic Club—there weren't that many of us there. In Philly, I mean. He was visiting there, from here."

"They say there are about a hundred of us here," Frieda interjected.

"Maybe. Anyway, he was my parents' age then, and I was barely twenty. In his fifties, in fact. But he was very good looking, and just out of a divorce. And rich, besides. And in short, I fell for him. I don't know—maybe he fell for me too. He acted like it. I guess I was flattered. I didn't think I had much of a chance . . ."

"And it turned out, you didn't," said Frieda.

"Turned out I didn't. But anyway—to make a long story short—we got together, but my parents probably never knew. Sometimes I thought my mother suspected, but it never came up. I moved here, with his help. He set me up in an apartment, and put me to work in one of his businesses. I was a receptionist there, too. I was perfectly content—I believed we would get married some day."

"Mama, you said you'd make it short. Didn't she?" Appealing to me. "Didn't she just say that?"

"She did, but I'm enjoying the story, long or short," I said.

"Okay," Ann continued. "I'll get to the point. So, then when Frieda came, I'll admit I went through a bad period. I finally figured out that we wouldn't marry, even though he always took care of us. Financially, I mean. Except for a couple of very hard years, when he was getting married to Christie. That's his wife. Last I heard . . ."

"Mama," Frieda said as she got up. She started gathering the salad plates and the wine glasses.

"Okay, okay. Then I got that letter from Whitman Stacy. That's the law firm I work for, now. Frieda and I had to go down there. Azad had set up a trust for Frieda, making me and Stan

46

Stacy—one of the lawyers—trustees. Until she's twenty-one, when she takes it over. I could decide how to spend the income, and even how to invest the money, as long as I could show Stan it was in Frieda's best interest. I had to sign a settlement saying I'd never sue Azad, which I was happy to do, since Stan said this was a better settlement than the courts would ever give us, and I believed him."

"So, any trouble convincing Mr. Stacy this condo was good for Frieda?" I asked, realizing only then that my question might be taken to be a bit pointed.

"I convinced him," said Frieda cheerfully, bringing in a big lovely-smelling bowl of seafood in a thick broth, and setting it in front of me—clams in their shells, deep-sea clams out of theirs, squid, lumps of fish. Crab meat. Seaweed and something else green. A lot of work, I knew, and careful preparation. "But," continued Frieda, "I really wanted to be sure that Ann would have a place to stay, if I leave in four or five years."

Frieda went back twice to get bowls for Ann and herself, and Ciabatta bread and unsalted butter and some other things. Meanwhile Ann set out new wine glasses, into which she poured from a new bottle of wine, which I asked to see. It was a Viognier, which I hadn't expected.

But it turned out to be a perfect, and surprising, accompaniment to the Cioppino, which I'd remembered was the name of the fish stew. The stew was spicy, as promised. And the wine, after quite a dry starting taste, had a very fruity finish. Sweet isn't my thing, but this kind of sweet, and icy cold, was exactly what the almost fiery broth required. Who would have guessed? I was filled with admiration for the cook, and she must have seen that, when I looked at her and shook my head in wonder. I realized at once that my head-shake could have been interpreted as a sort of rejection, so I changed it to a nod, which made her laugh—and blush! She was almost excessively pleased at my reaction.

I realized, with a strange mixture of apprehension and pleasure of my own, that my response had been important to her. Who did she think I was?

Eating the Cioppino required a certain amount of concentration, so that's what we did. There was some small talk, but it felt most natural just to eat in silence, with occasional irrelevant comments, and with the cool music in the background. The only slight distraction was that Frieda kept glancing at her watch. Nevertheless it was, in spite of that oddity, and of the ordinariness of the occasion, an exalting experience.

And then, as we finished, the second most surprising incident of the evening occurred.

I heard the honk of a car horn out front. "It's him," said Frieda, and jumped up, almost knocking her chair over. She ran around to me, and gave me a hug from behind. "Thanks for coming," she said. "I have to go—concert. Death Metal."

"I told her it was rude to have a late date tonight," said Ann.

"I'm sorry," said Frieda. "But I know you'll enjoy the rest of your evening. See you soon!" And she was off, down the hall.

"When will you be back?" called Ann.

"Don't know. Don't wait up." Then the door slammed.

I was open-mouthed.

"Boyfriend," explained Ann. "Parking's a problem around here, so he just honks."

"I see," I said. I sat, thoroughly bewildered.

"Paul?" said Ann. I looked at her. She just sat quietly for a moment. Longer. I thought maybe she wouldn't say anything else. And I hoped she wouldn't. My emotional state was close to shock, and at least I was looking at her, which I hoped would pass for a communication until I could recover enough to communicate. But then she spoke.

"Paul, you know she brought you here for me."

"What?" I said.

She repeated her statement. I had to struggle to make sense of it. Finally it reminded me of something that had happened earlier in our relationship, a long time before. Two weeks. "I guess she does that a lot," I said.

"A lot? No. You're the first. The only one."

"But when I first met you—saw you—in the restaurant, in the mall—you said it was a 'bad habit' of hers."

She had to think another moment about that. Then she laughed—a sort of bubbly sound, like her daughter's, but lower-pitched. "Oh, yes, she does check out a lot of men, I guess. Although I hope she's finally listened to me, and stopped. Anyway, you're the only one who made it through the interview." And she laughed again.

So, it *was* an interview! I couldn't remember it, in detail. I'd decided it was too embarrassing to remember. I wondered what I could possibly have done right.

"What did I do right?" I asked.

"You must have been yourself," she said. "That would have been the most important thing to her. She said you're very lonely. And that you're not good at meeting people. Socially. I'm not either. She thinks we both need her help. She's very good at it."

"So she said," I said.

We were gazing at each other now, Ann and I, full in each others' faces. I seemed to feel that a steady gaze was a way to disguise the fact I was still a little stunned, but I also found her face a comfortable place to rest my eyes. I don't know why she felt comfortable just looking at me. But that's what we did, for a long time, without words.

Finally she said, "You can look at them, you know."

"Look at what?" I said, although I was afraid I knew what she meant, and my quick glance down at her chest must have confirmed that I knew.

"My breasts. You've been wanting to look at them all evening."

"Oh, no, Ann. You don't have to . . ."

"I know I don't have to," she said, as she reached around to her back, to unzip something. "Of course I don't have to." Then she pulled her blouse thing up over her head, and dropped it to the floor.

50

It had the same affect as a slap in the face—it's the kind of thing that makes you forget everything else until you've attended to it. Even the previous disturbances of the evening.

"Won't you get cold?" I said, still staring at her eyes. I did manage to take in the breasts as well, as they swayed out of their enclosure. But I couldn't look directly at them. I continued staring at her face. I have no idea why. Maybe I was embarrassed for her.

She pushed back her dishes, giving her a little room on the table in front of her.

"Look at them," she said, quietly. It suddenly occurred to me that they could go back into hiding as easily as they came out, and how hard it might be to coax them out again if I let that happen. So I looked.

And she just sat, her arms lying on the table, one hand on top of the other. The combination of her large breasts and her hairy forearms had a most intense and confusing effect that I couldn't begin to understand. And the fact that she was letting me look at them. *Making* me look at them.

After a while she got up and moved her chair over from behind the table. I watched her every motion, and noticed once more her small long waist, her wide hips still encased in their trousers. I also saw, for the first time, her slightly pudgy tummy. And I saw that a thin line of hair emerged from the top of her pants and dwindled out halfway up to her breasts. Then she sat down again, crossing her ankles, and laid her wrists on her thighs.

She'd moved to give me a better view! No dissembling, no pretense. She was simply displaying herself. Selected parts of herself.

I felt that I was being called upon to do something, to make a move. And some movement of mine must have signaled that.

"Just look," she said.

I relaxed, and watched the quiet, still display, waiting for the next instruction. That's what she seemed to want me to do, and doing what she wanted relieved me of any responsibility for what I did.

And so, the first thing that I gave up for the evening was my impatience, and then my embarrassment, as I slowly came to appreciate what was being done for me, for whatever reason. Followed, as a sort of afterthought, by my feeling that I should try to control things. Control had been taken over by a higher power. Ann's body. Definitely a higher power.

And as I gazed, the room receded into the background, along with the rest of my life.

"Frieda said you'd be able to do this," said Ann.

I had no idea what to say, so I didn't say anything. Nor did I really know what she meant. But after a while, I suppose when she decided I was ready, Ann got up and walked over to me. It was as though her breasts were swaying and floating through the air towards me, and filling my whole vision. She stood close in front of me a while, then she placed her arms on both sides of my neck, with her fingers behind my head. Bringing her arms forward brought

her breasts fully together. I could feel her arm hair on my ea
She nestled my face into her cleavage, then started rocking my
gently forward and back.

I enjoyed that for a while, nuzzling my face around. Then
on impulse, I put my hands on her wide hips. Fortunately that was
acceptable; it caused her to embrace my head beneath her breasts
and move her hips closer, allowing my hands to reach around her
butt. It was well padded, but I could feel the muscles fluctuating
underneath. I rubbed my hands around on it, grabbing gently every
few seconds, when my hands reached the place I must have felt was
appropriate for grabbing, while she set up the rhythm for my grabs
by squeezing my head against her. A strange thing to do, but almost
as though we'd rehearsed it.

We did that for quite a long time. Then, just as I was
deciding what I wanted to do next, she did something. I should have
known it wasn't up to me. She stepped back, taking my hands, and
pulled me to my feet. She continued pulling me back to her chair
and sat down. Then she very slowly unbuttoned my shirt, and left it
hanging open. "No undershirt?" she asked. "Won't you get cold?"
Again, her casual little laugh.

"It's a warm evening," I said. She was one to talk.

Now she was undoing my trousers. She showed no concern
about destroying any moods or spoiling any spells. Or shocking me
silly. No hurry at all. She pulled down my trousers and underpants
at the same time, and smiled as my penis bounced up like a spring.
She took it and held it in her hand, looking at it.

"I'm glad it's big," she said.

Didn't Frieda say it would be big? I almost said, but fortunately caught myself. Instead I said, "It's not particularly big." Unless, of course, she meant it was hard. It was definitely hard.

"It's big enough," she said, chuckling. "It's not small."

I left it at that.

She sort of caressed it for a while with her hands, then put it in her mouth, and caressed it some more, somehow, with the back of her tongue and her throat. I noticed that everything we did, we kept on doing for a much longer time than I remembered from those long-ago occasions, when I was younger and less patient and more in charge. But finally, when I became concerned that I was going to finish long before I wanted to, I backed off and reversed her last major maneuver, pulling her to her feet and over to my chair, where I sat again.

And pulled down her slacks, complete with underpants. It was a struggle, getting her slacks over her hips and bottom, but the waist was all elastic so I managed.

I thought I was prepared for what I saw, but it still took me aback. I was like an explorer crossing a meadow, coming to the top of a hill, and expecting more meadow in the valley on the other side. But what I saw instead was a deep jungle. I had the unnerving sensation that I'd stopped just in time before tumbling over a cliff and falling down into it. The trail of hair leading to the jungle was modest enough, and in fact her tummy otherwise had only a fine sort of fuzz on it. But beneath that, heaped up between her legs and

54

spreading down over her thighs, was an extravagance I hadn't foreseen.

Startled, I looked up into her face. She was smiling, and my expression, which must have had some alarm in it, brought out her melodious laugh again. Then she pulled my head back into what she must have previously found to be a comfortable position, held gently, sideways against her tummy, just below her breasts. In a daze, I returned to embracing her butt. It was different this time, because of the soft fur nearly covering it, which led me to add a sort of stroking movement to my grabbing, as though I were petting an animal.

And after a while, she followed suit, as before, with rhythmic motions that responded to mine, her hips pushing whenever I squeezed her butt. She spread her feet a little, bringing her breasts down so that my face was between them, and increased her tempo. I was sitting on the edge of my chair; but at some point I was pulled right off, onto my knees, on the floor. Now her vast bush was pushed against my naked chest, and outclassing it with no contest. I felt very strongly that the time had come for a final development in our activities, although by now I knew not to try to anticipate the exact details of that development. And as usual, we just continued with what we were doing longer than I expected; and in spite of my growing feeling of urgency, once again I didn't really want it to end.

And then, another surprise: I felt a little shudder where she was pressing against me, and she stopped moving. I looked up at her, and this time she wasn't smiling. Her mouth was half open, and her eyelids half closed, and I felt a brief moment of slight alarm; but then she brought her feet back together, and composed her expression, and stepped back.

And in her eyes I could see a hint of—of what? Could it have been *guilt*? I half expected her to say she was sorry, although I would have had no idea what for.

But she didn't say that. What she said was, "It's been a long time."

"So it has, " I said. Only later did I realize that she must have been apologizing for going ahead with her orgasm without regard for me. She needn't have worried.

She took my hands and pulled me to my feet, and out into the hall. "Let's get under the covers," she said. "Before we get too cold." And indeed, I did feel the cool air on the wet spot on my chest, as she led me into the bedroom.

In bed she rolled over, facing me, and I realized I hadn't kissed her yet. I made up for that immediately; and we kissed for a long time, of course. And I managed to get her nipples between my lips, and lick her tits, while she held onto my penis and felt my butt, making me grateful for the squats I'd been doing at the gym.

But a new worry was bothering me. "What about pregnancy, Ann?" I asked. "And disease?"

"I started back on the pill a week ago, when Frieda told me she liked you. And she said you didn't have any diseases. She said you hadn't had sex for a long time."

"Okay Ann, look. I know you have lots of faith in Frieda, and I can see why. But how could she possibly know about my diseases?"

"Are you saying she was wrong? That you do have some?"

"I . . . no. I don't have any diseases. Not that kind, anyway."

"So, she was right."

"Well, uh . . . yes. She was right." I saw it was pointless to continue in opposition.

"I don't have any either," she said, sort of rolling again, onto her back, and pulling me on top of her.

Our lovemaking was slow and gentle and very familiar, even though we had only just met. The whole thing was almost miraculously comfortable and without anxiety, except that she seemed particularly anxious to please me. And I was pleased, beyond any fantasies I'd ever had. And I'd thought Frieda was a witch. She must have been trained by her mother.

After we'd finished and were sitting up, leaning against the headboard, it occurred to me that I knew, in part at least, how she'd done it.

"Ann, all that looking you had me doing when we started. I didn't know what it was for. But now I think I do. I feel that I've got to know you very quickly. Or some important things about you. How did you know to do that?" Immediately, I realized I could have made a big mistake. I didn't really want to know how she knew.

But once again, she navigated around the danger, as she'd done already several times that evening. "Oh, I was doing something else, too," she said.

"Something else?"

"Well, it's true that I've always felt more at ease with a man who has looked at me," she said. "And I was trying to get past some of the things that cause trouble between lovers. You know, right at first. But also, there was Frieda."

"Frieda?"

"She's quite a captivating young woman. I wouldn't have been surprised if she had captivated you. I had to get you off of her and onto me."

Once again I was open-mouthed, but I was able to mumble, "You certainly did that."

"Anyway, you'll have to admit she got us going," Ann continued. "Now it's up to you if we want to keep going."

I started to tell her I wanted to keep going with her—right then, in fact—but decided it wasn't wise to rush these things. Instead I invited her to a jazz session at Alex's Blue Room the next night. And she accepted, I thought, with satisfying enthusiasm.

"Now, Paul," she said. "Would you like some dessert?"

"Dessert! Really! What's for dessert?"

"Grapes and cheese," she said.

Three Hairy Women

Three Hairy Women

III: APRIL LOVE

*   1   *

It was on a Friday, early in January midway through her fifteenth year, that April Ahlberg was brought to an understanding of who she really was.

Her revelation came in two parts. At first she felt the two parts were contradictory. But then her junior high school phys ed instructor said something that clicked them together into a clear, simple motto for her young life.

She was standing by the swimming pool, waiting for the class to start with the rest of the female component of the ninth grade, some fifty girls at slightly different stages of pubescence. They were all wearing the same bathing suit, or they looked the same—off-white nearly shapeless single-piece things they'd all had to buy, or which the school bought for them if they could prove they couldn't afford them. The suits came in a few standard sizes, and April was told that her size was med / med, which meant medium height medium girth. When she tried it on, she was sure it was wrong, since it hung on her like a bag; but her teacher said it was as close a fit as she'd be able to get.

The suits didn't look shapeless on all the girls, although all the girls complained about them. April was fully aware, before the term started, that some of the girls in her class already had well-developed chests and bottoms. But she'd never thought about it much, because many of her classmates, like her best friend Angie, were coming along as slowly as she was. She and Angie grumbled and laughed about it from time to time. April's mother kept telling her she'd have her day, and her big brother Ned, two years older than she was, would always introduce her as his "cute little sister." Ned was already the starting quarterback on the high school team, and was good-looking and popular, and April just believed that what he said had to be true. He was her close friend, maybe even closer than Angie. She couldn't remember a week when they hadn't gone swimming together, some weeks two or three times, at the big Vesey Park pool, and he habitually got her into his basketball games with his buddies. She knew he wouldn't lie to her.

And there was also Robbie. Robbie was Ned's best friend, except for April. He was a wide receiver on the team, and he was also very handsome and very tall. And he was always nice to her. Sometimes he flirted with her, winking and saying things like "Hi, girlfriend," or "Bye-bye, Cutie." April told Angie she planned to marry him, and they giggled about it.

But it was true. She knew he liked her. She knew as much about sports and the pro players' names and records as he did. And if anything, more about music, which he was *really* into. Robbie and Ned mainly liked hard rock, especially Metallica. But April had discovered King Crimson before the boys had heard of them, thanks to a mention by a teacher. And she had coaxed them into listening to Kris Kristofferson before his songs were really popular, and even to Leonard Cohen, who had become her favorite after another of her teachers had recommended him.

And there was the dancing. Not that April had ever danced with Robbie. April hadn't even liked disco all that much when it first came in—until, that is, she and Angie talked April's mother into taking them to the Saturday night dances at the Catholic church socials, which welcomed anybody, even non-Catholics. The two girls would dance together to "Dancing Queen," and April would imagine that Robbie had come in without her seeing him, and was watching her. She knew that he was impressed with her energy and style, but that he could also see through those things to the real April underneath.

As time went by, and she and Robbie never got into conversations—just the two of them—April even rehearsed little things to do and say, to let him know how she felt.

But that was before all her classmates, along with her, put on their one-piece suits and their white rubber caps, taking turns in the little stalls in the dressing room. Then they went, otherwise naked, and stood around the pool, looking at each other.

They didn't stare, of course. But they glanced. And some of them did stare—she noticed a couple of them staring at her. But she ignored them. She didn't really know those particular girls. Without staring herself, she noticed that almost every girl there had breasts. Some were full, some barely showed, and others you couldn't tell if they were really breasts because the girls were fat.

And then April noticed something else, or imagined she did. The fat girls, generally, just stood still and looked straight ahead, except for Veronica, who was noisy and was always moving anyway. The skinny, nearly flat-chested girls were also, most of them, just standing still with a dull look in their eyes. Most of the lively ones—the wiggly, laughing, happy girls—were the curvy ones.

As April took it all in, she found herself wondering if it could be true, that all these girls were taking their shapes as seriously as they seemed to be. How could they be making so much of it? She knew, of course, that lots of girls were very concerned with their looks—their hair, their clothes, their skin. April herself worried when she got pimples on her face, and put medicine on them every night. But shapes? Girls come in all different sizes and shapes!

As for April herself, she had no breasts at all. Nothing that showed, and what didn't show would have been an embarrassment. She stood still and stared straight ahead. So did Angie, standing next to her. But April, when she glanced, could see Angie's little protrusions, pushing out the stretchy not-quite-white material of her bathing suit. Coming along nicely. April felt almost betrayed.

At first April's mother described her as a "late starter." "Don't worry, Hon," she said. "You'll catch up."

But the hair told a different story. April had started growing pubic hair before Angie, as April found out when her reference to it,

which she intended as another bonding secret between them, met with a blank stare. Soon after that the light brown hair started on her legs and underarms. Some other girls in April's class had more than the usual hair on their legs, but it had disappeared soon after it became noticeable. So April wasn't surprised when her mother called her into the bathroom, presented her with her new razor, and gave her a lesson. "Part of our lot in life," she said, with a sigh and smile of resignation.

But then the hair on her forearms also became a little more noticeable than was acceptable. Her mother pretended to ignore it, but April noticed her looking at her arms, from time to time, with a worried expression.

Finally one Friday evening after Ned had gone out with Robbie and his other buddies, April's mother threw her hands in the air. "I'm sorry," she said. "It'll just have to go. You can't keep on like that. It's your father's fault. Ned's the same. Of course, it's fine on him. I can't believe I fell for your father for that reason. I really believe, if he hadn't been so hairy, I'd have seen all his faults ahead of time and we wouldn't be alone now."

So April had to start shaving her arms as well. Shaving was beginning to take up a big portion of her week. Fortunately she could make up for it by not spending as much time on her makeup as some of the girls had started to do.

When her period began, about the same time as most of the girls in her class, her mother had to stop making her "late starter" excuses. April could feel her mother's disappointment. For Ned, she was still the "Cute Sis." She wondered when he would notice that she wasn't really so cute. And Robbie.

It took three days in the swimming class for April herself to notice. That is, to face what ordinary observation had been telling her for a year or more. Unfortunately she had managed to ignore it until now, so that when her life-changing Friday arrived, she had to face it all at once.

The girls were to swim three times a week, alternating with the boys, who took the longer sessions on Tuesdays and Thursdays. The first Monday was spent in trials, when the girls who said they could swim had to prove it by swimming a length. There was still plenty of time for standing and looking at each other, while girls splashed their way to the end of the pool. When it was April's turn, she didn't swim as fast as she could. She never liked to show off. But still she came in a long way ahead of the girls in the other lanes. As April climbed out, Miss Collins, the younger of the phys ed teachers, walked over to her. "Take after you brother, don't you," she said.

April didn't get what she meant right away. "Pardon?" she asked.

"Aren't you Ned Ahlberg's sister?"

"Yes ma'am," said April, a little confused and embarrassed. She resisted the impulse to look down at herself, to see if she'd left anything showing.

"Athletic ability seems to run in the family," said Miss Collins.

66

"Oh . . . oh," said April, relieved. "I guess so, maybe. Thanks." And she went back to her place.

On the Wednesday, the class was separated into learners, who went to the learners' pool, and swimmers. The swimmers were divided into four groups, paired off into "buddies" to keep their eyes on each other, and rotated for practice in the various strokes and basic safety. April's buddy was Marcia, a tall girl, not particularly curvy except for her big breasts. April had suddenly started noticing such things. She'd already *noticed* them, actually, for a while, but now for the first time she was paying attention to them.

Then came Friday.

April's group was to be a team for the water polo, which only the best swimmers were allowed to play. It was right at the beginning, while they were standing around the pool for role call, that the cruel message the other girls' bodies had been sending her finally broke through to April, along with lots of other things she'd been willfully ignoring. Her mother's worried face. Ned's increasing neglect, ever since he met Helen at Vesey Park. The fact that Robbie never sought her out for conversation, just the two of them. Everything April had been trying to disregard about herself jumped up into her face and shouted at her. And what it shouted was this: "You're a stick!"

A stick. She was a stick! It wouldn't change. She was developing, but she wouldn't develop any feminine beauties. She was a hairy stick. A shaved hairy stick.

And that meant something, to be only that. Something awful. The pretty, sexy girls were right to be happy. They all had boyfriends now, another fact April had been ignoring. April had just assumed there were people who loved her. They were the people she loved—her mother, her brother, Angie, maybe even Robbie. Maybe some other friends—other students she liked, whom she would get to know better during the term.

But Ned also loved Helen, at least for now. Robbie didn't have anybody, as far as she knew, although sometimes he double-dated with Ned. April just thought they were all buddies.

But now she saw, suddenly, that Robbie wouldn't love her in that way. When it came to boys and girls, looks were everything. She suddenly saw that she even loved Robbie for *his* looks. And because he was nice to her. Robbie would never *want* her. She wouldn't be his dancing queen.

It was, of course, just an ordinary teenage heartbreak. Scarcely even that. Something like that must happen to most girls— probably to some of them around that same pool on that same day. And the world accommodates many girls in far worse situations, of course. There are girls whom nobody ever loves.

But for that reason people might too readily dismiss the suffering of girls like April, who because they have always had love, have let themselves be encouraged, and aren't prepared when they have to face their big disappointment by themselves.

However, that was just the first of the two revelations April had about herself on that Friday.

April walked along with the other good swimmers toward the deep end, in a state of shock and confusion, following her "buddy," Marcia, whom she'd seen around, but didn't know. She wanted to leave, to go off by herself and let it all work itself out. But instead she had to play water polo! It seemed very unfair. She couldn't do it. And then, as Miss Collins was explaining the basic starting rules of the game and dividing the teams, she decided she *wouldn't* do it. She would pretend to be sick. Maybe she would double up in a fetal position on the edge of the pool. Close her eyes and refuse to respond. She felt that would be a suitable thing to do.

So overwhelming was her new discovery that she found herself fantasizing that the group she was in resulted from a division, not between good and poor swimmers, but between attractive and unattractive girls. She was in the ugly group. What would happen to them? They would be discarded, but how? Could they maybe stay together somehow, go off by themselves together?

In the midst of her fantasy, Miss Collins told them to jump into the pool, and when the other girls jumped, April did too. The jolt of the cool water purged her mind, leaving it blank. She held onto the ledge with the other girls—the water here was too deep to stand on the bottom. She noticed that some of the girls now had round red discs on their caps. She'd seen them stick them on, but hadn't paid attention. April didn't have one, so that must be the other team.

"Now, if you get really tired, during the game, you can kick to the edge and grab the rail," Miss Collins was saying. "But remember, as long as you're hanging there, your team will be a player short."

April was concocting her next plan. For sure, she wasn't playing water polo. She didn't even know how. She would just tread water—sort of paddle around. As the game got under way, that's what most of the girls were doing anyway. The red-patch girls were throwing a white ball to each other. Every now and then Miss Collins would blow her whistle, and shout something, and something would happen. April wasn't sure what. One of the opposing girls managed to throw the ball at the net, but it fell short and the goalkeeper got it.

Now it was April's team that was passing the ball around, but April paddled over close to the edge where she wouldn't have to catch it. The chlorine smell and the water splashing in her face were reminding her of something—of the summers in the Vesey Park pool with Ned. That's where she'd learned to swim. Happier times. The rock music and the cold drinks. Last summer, Ned chatting up Helen, who was a lifeguard there. Helen was a very curvy girl. April totally approved, felt good for her brother and his new girlfriend, even if it meant she was getting less attention herself. Some day, she'd have . . .

Suddenly, April felt a surge of anger. Anger was so rare for her that at first she didn't recognize it. She just knew that she was having a very strong feeling, and that she needed to do

70

something. She wanted to scream, but didn't. She wanted to cry. Maybe she started crying.

It wouldn't be recognized by anyone that day, but in fact, April was about to have a tantrum.

"April!" shouted Marcia. April looked. Marcia had the ball. She threw it at her! April caught it.

Then she did scream. She let out a shriek, and at the same time she gave a huge scissor kick, which lifted her above the other girls. She was a long way from the net, but still she heaved the ball at it, using both arms. The goalkeeper managed to raise her own arms, but not high enough. The ball surged into the top of the net.

April looked around. Everyone was staring at her. Even Miss Collins.

Finally Miss Collins unfroze herself. "Nice shot, April," she said, and blew her whistle. The other phys ed teacher, the older one, who for some reason everyone called "Coach"—Coach Kemp—had come over and retrieved the ball from the net. She threw it to Miss Collins.

"Now, listen!" said Miss Collins. "You saw how April did it, she kicked herself up where she could get a clear shot. Connie— or anybody, when you want to *block* a shot—you have to do the same thing. You have to watch the player with the ball, when she starts to take a shot, you do the same thing, you kick yourself up where you can block it. Right, coach?"

"Right," said Coach Kemp.

"Okay Connie?" said Miss Collins. "Okay everybody?" She whistled again, and threw the ball to the red-capped girl furthest from the goal, and the goalkeepers changed positions. April noticed that the opposing goalkeeper, Connie, just went over to the edge and hung there.

"Way to shoot, April" shouted Marcia.

But April wasn't finished. When an opposing girl passed the ball to a player near her, April saw it coming and, giving another scissor kick, she lunged over and caught the ball at the same time as the other girl. Both girls had their hands on the ball, but the other girl was so surprised that April was able to wrench it from her. She was about to try another shot, but then she heard Marcia shouting again.

"April! April! Here!"

The cry was so urgent that April looked around. Marcia was holding her hands out for the ball, and gesturing with her head at the side of the pool. April didn't see what she was gesturing at, but she threw her the ball anyway, just before the girl she'd just stolen it from splashed nearly on top of her. April backed away. She was beginning to think again. Her mad wild shot at the net had turned out better than she now saw it should have. She now wanted to make her next shot too.

She saw Marcia paddle backwards a couple of yards, and then, to her surprise, she threw her the ball again. April caught it and turned back toward the goal, to be confronted by her opponent, who was waving her arms wildly and splashing a lot. April did

72

her kick again, launching herself back and up—but then she saw every red-patched girl in the pool, nearly, loft into the air, arms up and waving, to block her shot.

So she didn't take it. As she sank back into the water, in the same movement, she flipped over and did a surface dive.

All of the noise was abruptly muffled. Her move was an intuitive one—something she had learned to do to get away from the big boys when they were chasing her. But now she realized she had a battle to stay down, because the ball kept trying to pull her back to the surface. She managed to get it under her, and kick back toward the bottom, as she blew some air out of her lungs. She had to kick frantically just to stay under.

She started directing herself toward the goal. The feet of the other players dangled above her. When she was about halfway to the wall, she realized she wasn't going to make it all the way. But she kept going and got a couple more kicks in.

Finally she turned upward and gave a hard final kick, breaking the surface between two opponents, and taking in a big gulp of air. Then she screamed again and propelled the ball around the side of the defender in front of her, toward the right side of the net. She saw the goalkeeper go up with her arms outstretched in defense, but the ball brushed beside her, into the goal.

"Do you have to make so much noise?" said one of the opposing girls. April knew to ignore such comments when playing sports, and she ignored it. But she noticed that this question seemed particularly silly. Couldn't this girl see that April wasn't a nice, pretty, quiet girl, like her?

The girls on April's own team were clapping. Miss Collins blew her whistle.

"Miss Collins, was that legal?" one of the opposing girls shouted. "What April just did?"

"Grab the rail," said Miss Collins. Everyone paddled over to the side. "Coach?" she said. "Was it legal?"

"No, it wasn't," said Coach Kemp, smiling. "You have to keep the ball above water. But that was a good try, April. And the shot was legal. More legal than it had to be." She laughed. "She did it with one hand. That's another rule—you have to handle the ball with one hand. Everybody except the goalkeeper. So, April's first shot would be illegal too, in most games."

April didn't know how to feel. She could have got angry again. She was still on edge. They hadn't told her! But maybe she just hadn't listened. Not that she would have done it different, even if she'd known.

Or she could have got depressed. That was closer to how she wanted to feel. But she didn't get any way, right away.

"But we usually suspend the two-hand rule for you girls," continued Coach Kemp, "since your hands aren't big enough yet. Still, it's possible, even with your hands. April's second shot proved that, right?"

Some of April's team clapped again.

"See, we've found that if you learn the rules as you go, you'll remember them better and you'll know what they're for," said Coach Kemp. "That's what we're doing now. Just playing around, having a little fun, getting the feel of the game. So, carry on. One-hand rule is suspended a while longer."

They carried on. April's team was credited with one point for her two semi-illegal goals. As the other girls were paddling out into the pool, Marcia paddled over to April. "Let's get a little closer to the net," she said, panting between sentences. "I'll get you the ball . . . Or somebody will . . . You make like you're gonna shoot—you kick up and everything . . . But don't shoot. Flip the ball to me instead . . . Okay?"

April nodded. She'd calmed down a little now. She thought she could see what Marcia was getting at. And so, when someone passed the ball to April, she rose up, holding the ball back to throw it. All the defenders went up too. But April dropped the ball into Marcia's waiting hands, and Marcia immediately kicked up and shot, while all the defenders were still dropping down. In the ball went, with no defending hands close.

April felt a little stirring of . . . something. A good feeling. Almost a tiny joy. The kind she used to feel playing with Ned before he became a star and didn't have much time to play with her any more.

The game continued for another twenty minutes. The other team learned quickly, with the help of Miss Collins' advice, and neither April nor Marcia came up with any more tricks. Still, the final score—although it turned out the teachers had trouble remembering—was 3 to 1 with April's team on top. April and Marcia had scored all their points.

As they were walking to the showers, where they would rinse off with their bathing suits still on, Coach Kemp stopped April. "Competitive, aren't you?" she said with a smile.

"I guess so," said April. She started to say, "You mean, like my brother?" But didn't.

"How would you like to swim with the big girls?"

April didn't know what she meant, which must have showed, because Coach Kemp explained. "The high school team. They train here afternoons, Mondays and Wednesdays. It would mean some schedule changes for you, but I could arrange that. Anyway, think about it."

"Okay," said April, and started to walk away. But then she stopped, and said, "Coach Kemp?"

"Yes?"

"How about Marcia? She's my buddy. Can she come too?"

Coach Kemp laughed. "Well, not because she's your buddy. But in fact, I had that in mind. *I'll* have to think about that one."

As April walked into the dressing room, she found her anger had pretty much ebbed. She felt a little better than she had halfway through that day's revelations, although it still hadn't settled in what the second half meant. But then something happened that would clarify things for her, a little.

Miss Collins was shouting to the girls. "Hey, I'm tired of all that complaining about the bathing suits. Here, it doesn't matter what you look like. All that matters is what you can do." Half the girls were in the showers, and didn't hear what she said.

But April heard.

*   2   *

April and Marcia had little trouble swimming with the big girls. Marcia was a big girl herself, although she was a little gangly and clumsy; and it turned out she'd done a lot of swimming at her country club pool. And April, after all, had done a lot of swimming with the big *boys.*

Of course, they had much to learn. But the high school girls let them learn, mainly by getting on with their own training and ignoring them, or by laughing at them when they did something stupid. Coach Kemp, who was the swimming coach for the high school girls, would occasionally shout a word of advice to them, but she also mainly left them alone.

It turned out that the big girls were all swimmers on the swimming team, not just polo players, and that's what April and Marcia did too. Coach Kemp assigned each of them to a different senior girl, and told them to do as much of the senior's workout as they could. "Just stay out of their way," she warned. And then she would change their assignments every few weeks, so they could learn all the different competition strokes, and develop a sense of their most promising specialties. Marcia liked the backstroke—because, she said, she didn't have to worry as much about breathing—and April the butterfly. April was a fast freestyler too, but so were a couple of older girls, so she chose the less popular niche to improve her chances of making the team next year.

But April's real specialty was water polo. The polo team practiced only once a week, late on Fridays, and April and Marcia got to play on the "B" squad. April's initial successes in the sport had given her an attachment to it, which was soon reinforced by her natural ability at controlling her aim of shots and passes, a talent her brother Ned was also exhibiting, in a different sport, as high school quarterback. Of course, Ned's ability was well known around town, while April's was known only among the girl swimmers and their coach.

And that suited April. "Here, all that matters is what you can do." But it wasn't that way everywhere. It had been burned into April's subconscious that elsewhere, in the big world out there, other things mattered more. And she'd decided that "here" was where she wanted to live.

And she knew intuitively that the big world outside was dangerous to her newly discovered, fragile little island of female swimmers. She knew it was so, because she'd only recently left that big world herself. And because her mother, who still had more influence over her than any other person, still lived in it, and still tried to impose its values and ways on her.

She hadn't exactly admitted to herself that her mother was a threat to her. But she could feel herself cringing whenever Mother commented, however casually, on her new "hobby." "Butterfly! Honey, are you sure? What about that girl on television—I'm sure it was butterfly—don't you remember? She won the race, and was getting out of the pool, and we all saw that her shoulders were huge! Ned said, 'What a monster!' Or something like that. You remember. I'm sure it was butterfly!"

Or another time, "Honey, if you have to have a sport—I mean, I never needed one, but if you *have* to—I want you to find something else when you get to high school. Something less . . . you know, less *messy*. Just think what that water, all that splashing around, will do to your makeup! I know, you don't wear it now, but I'm sure you'll want to soon. Anyway, most of those outdoor sports, all that sweating, are nothing but trouble. Even tennis. But swimming's the worst. What about golf? If you *have* to have a sport. I never needed one myself."

Mother was a successful real estate agent, and to hear her describe how she got her start, it was mainly due to her good looks when she was younger, and her shrewdness in using them to her advantage. "The wives will do most of the talking and ask most of the questions," she said. "And they'll be pleased if you just chat with them, as if you're their best friend. Share a few confidences. You know, about your personal likes and dislikes. Including some that aren't too favorable for that property, the one you're showing them. That'll get their trust. Try to find out if she has some strong opinions about what she wants. Usually it'll be a few simple things. The next property will be a perfect fit, if you plan it that way! Just become her friend. But don't forget—never forget—it's the husband who has the money. Throw in stuff about, you know, location and square footage and quality construction. And glance at him and smile when you do. But then start glancing and smiling when you don't, too. Just try not to let her see you do it too much. He'll think you go for him! Works every time."

April thought her mother's success could be better attributed to shrewdness than beauty. She was no beauty now, April thought. But she looked "nice." That is, she dressed like every other "business and professional" woman in town.

April had never argued with her mother about things like that, and she didn't start now, or not seriously. When she did argue, it was in an agreeable way. "Oh Mother," she would say. "Not all high school girl swimmers have big shoulders! Nancy Charleston doesn't, and she swims butterfly!" Or, "Some of the swimmers just put on more makeup after swimming. It's not that big a deal."

But she could feel that the disagreement went much deeper than that. After all, Mother wanted her *not* to do the very thing she'd realized she *had* to do. Train. Work out, hard. Harder than anybody else. One way or another, every day. And don't let anything distract her from that. Not even a mother's advice.

And it wasn't long before she could tell that her mother could feel their differences too. "April, really," she would say.

"Sometimes I get the feeling you just *don't care* how you look! Don't you *want* people to like you?"

But after a while she changed her message slightly. "Just look your best," she'd started to say. "That's all I ask of you." So, April would start trying to do a few things, like brushing her hair before she knew she would see her mother, or acting very pleased when her mother gave her a new girly blouse or skirt.

April's attitude displayed the extent of her alienation. Most teenagers would have quarreled with their mothers, but April was already distanced enough to know her mother was trying to do her best for her. Mother just didn't know what was best. April's spirit had already left home. She took her body with her, since she needed it. But when she didn't need it, she parked it at home, a sort of agreeable automaton, to appease her mother.

And finally Mother's arguments became less frequent, and her efforts less enthusiastic. Maybe she could see, as April herself did, that her daughter's case was hopeless. Nothing she did would make her pretty.

It wasn't that April had broken all ties with her mother. She couldn't have known how to do that, and things kept coming up to remind her of them. Her taste in music, for example, had always been closer to Mother's than to Ned's and Robbie's. She and Mother had especially shared a love for Crosby Stills and Nash, and the Eagles, and for *Bridge Over Troubled Water.* Mother had been amazed that there was no generation gap between herself and her daughter, as there had been between her, with her love for Elvis, and her parents, who were big band enthusiasts. When Mother brought home the new album *Rumors*, April was easily seduced into a whole evening of listening to it with her, over and over again, sipping cup after cup of hot apple cider. And experiencing a strong feeling that she was too young to recognize as nostalgia, for the times before she was separated from her mother.

Also, it wasn't that April really knew where she was going. She knew she was leaving. But the push wouldn't have been enough without some sort of pull, and she couldn't guess where swimming was pulling her. When she let herself think about it, she would be overcome by the strangeness of it. All her life she'd gone along with her mother's wishes, and with the fashions among her classmates, because that's what her mother wished her to do. She'd tried to copy the popular kids at school, saying she loved and "just hated" what they said they liked and disliked, and talking and dressing as they did. And as long as her mother and big brother and friends approved of her, she felt happy.

But she also felt empty, as though that collection of imitations, the clothes and appearance and manners and acceptable opinions and fears of disapproval, were all there was to her. They were clustered around a hollow space. There had never been anything inside that she could be sure was April.

Now it was different. Where the emptiness had been, something hard was growing. It was female, for sure. But it wasn't interested in her sexuality, and certainly not in boys. She

remembered with contempt the fantasies she'd had—not that

long ago—about Robbie. She'd imagined that he could see the "real April" inside her. Now she knew that the real April had been all on the surface. She'd been like one of those Easter eggs with the insides sucked out.

Above all, she wasn't interested in happiness. She didn't even didn't know whether or not she was happy because she didn't care. She'd tried happiness, and it hadn't worked. Now she had other concerns.

All the same, for her mother's sake April kept up the daily ritual of shaving her arms and legs. It wasn't difficult, because the high school girls did it in the shower—at least they did their legs. April did hers there too.

What happened with Angie was as disturbing as the distancing between April and her mother. April didn't intend to lose touch with her best friend, it just sort of happened. One night Angie telephoned to say she had something to show her, and that she was coming straight over. April hadn't seen Angie for a while, because with April's new schedule their paths didn't cross as regularly at school. And April had been intending to tell her about something she'd seen and heard recently, which had struck her as a kind of revelation. She found herself waiting for Angie with a touch of the old excitement that had always accompanied their sharing secrets.

When April opened the door, it seemed to her that Angie's eyes were glowing. Then she noticed the little chain around her neck, and that there was something hanging on it, under her blouse. April instinctively hugged her, and said, "You're happy about something, aren't you?" Angie pushed her back enough that she could pull out the little chain, to show her what was on it. A high school ring.

April knew what it meant, of course. Angie had a boyfriend. Somebody a little older.

"Oh, Angie!" said April, hugging her again. "Who is it?"

"Oh, it's Daniel," said Angie. Her tone suggested the inevitability of it all. Both of them had known Daniel for a long time. He was a nice boy, a junior at the high school.

"Oh Angie, I'm so happy for you!" said April, hugging her again. And she was. April had felt a little guilty about neglecting her friend.

"I haven't seen you for a long time, with your swimming and all," said Angie, as they went up to April's room, the cubbyhole for many of their most secret confessions. April's stuffed toys were still on the bed, as they'd always been, and the corkboard with clippings and Polaroid snapshots tacked to it, including some featuring Angie. "I've been meaning to tell you," Angie was saying. "We just started talking one day, after church, like we never had before. And one thing just led to another, you know? It was almost like talking to . . ."

"To me? He must be a very precious, sweet boy!" said April, and they both laughed. But April felt the clear substitution, the loss of intimacy between the two girls, and Angie noticed.

"It just happened, last night," said Angie. You're the first one I've told. I hadn't seen you for so long, I thought maybe you'd met . . . I mean, maybe . . ."

"No," said April, making a wry face. "Swimming just takes up all my time. And it's all girls, you know. But you know what I found out? I made the polo team—the *high school* team—starting in September! And Coach Kemp says I'll be a *starter*!"

"Oh, April!" said Angie, hugging her again. "That's wonderful!" April didn't tell her she'd known that for a month.

So they talked, remembering old conversations and laughing at the silly things they'd said when they were little girls. Angie talked as though she were an old settled married woman now, referring every few minutes to what Daniel says or to the bad habits he has. These boys. The two girls raided the refrigerator and drank some Hawaiian Punch for old times' sake. After a while, Angie had to go. Daniel would be coming to her house later. They hugged each other again and congratulated each other again, and Angie walked away.

April had decided not to tell her what she'd thought of telling her earlier.

It had to do with an old Disney cartoon film she'd seen, late at night by herself, a few nights before. Johnny Appleseed—a frontier character who walked the countryside, planting apple trees. She'd found it merely amusing at first, in an old Disney sort of way.

85

Then came the song. It was Johnny's song. It summarized his life.
It went like this:

> *Oh, the Lord is good to me*
> *And so I thank the Lord*
> *For giving me*
> *The things I need*
> *The sun, the rain,*
> *And the apple seed.*
> *The Lord is good to me.*

April didn't think she was listening. She felt no connection
with frontiersmen. But slowly, something about what Johnny's song
was saying made its way into her attention. He was thanking the
Lord for giving him what he needed. And what was that? Money?
Friends? Popularity? Good looks? Nice clothes? A companion?

No. He needed the sun. And the rain. And apple seeds.

He needed those things, April saw, because apple trees
needed them. He needed them to do his work. He didn't even think
of anything else. His work, not himself.

And then it occurred to April that that was her song too.

It seemed kind of silly, now, but only if she told somebody
else. How could she explain it to anyone else? She couldn't tell
Angie. Angie had found a *boyfriend*, and April had found . . . a
song.

She certainly couldn't tell Mother. Mother already suspected
that her daughter was a little crazy. Ned already had everything, and
didn't need to settle for just one thing, like work. And there was

nobody else she knew who might understand. Maybe Marcia. But she wasn't sure. Their relationship so far had been very congenial, but pretty much all business.

So she kept it to herself. But she, herself, had no doubts about it.

*   3   *

April did take one piece of her mother's advice. At this point, Mother was still trying to talk her into giving up swimming, and one of the reasons she came up with was that it took too much time, and so interfered with her studies.

April was incredulous. Mother had never been much of an advocate for studying. You had to pass, of course. But since it was looks and personality that really counted in the business and social worlds, studying too much was "counterproductive." And April had never been much for studying either, mainly because her mother and big brother weren't believers, but also because she'd always got good enough grades without it.

But this time she sensed that Mother had found a potent argument, whether or not she actually believed it, that she could use to get her way. So she decided she had to give studying a try. She started bringing her books home instead of leaving them in her school locker. Her aim at first was just to prove to her mother that she could swim *and* study. But slowly, it turned into something else.

On a less conscious level, April recognized schoolwork as a sort of vacant property, occupied neither by her mother nor older brother, just waiting to be claimed. They didn't want it, but it was said to have some value. It was something she could have as her own.

Besides, April was feeling the need for something more to do during the school year. More variety. Her entire social life was now the swimming team, and that occurred only during the appointed hours. She seldom saw the other swimmers at other times, and they were in high school anyway, and older. Ned was always gone somewhere these days, now that Mother had bought him a car, although he seemed still to sleep at home. Sometimes he would show up with Helen, or Robbie, but they wouldn't stay long. Mother was bustling about as usual. April didn't see Angie any more, and the occasional chats with other students in the halls didn't amount to much.

So classes were April's only daily occupation, other than workouts. And oddly, she'd started getting interested in some of them, largely because they'd become a proportionately bigger part of her life. Particularly algebra and science. And a little bit in "social studies," which this term was American history.

It wasn't easy, since April had never studied much before. It felt very strange to be sitting for hours in the evenings, at the little table she'd converted into a desk in her room, working through problems. Or reading propped up in her bed, nestled among her soft toys, her yellow highlighter held clumsily at the ready.

She left her door open, since the whole point was for her mother to see her. But that meant that the noises her mother or brother were making, whether talking with each other, or on the telephone, or watching TV, were distracting. Besides, she was usually tired from her workout. Her mind would wander.

But the self-denying self-discipline she'd been imposing on herself in her workouts spilled over into her study time, and kept her going.

At first she didn't think that studying made any difference. But then she started noticing that she was looking forward to classes. The reason was that, for the first time, she understood everything that was going on, or if she didn't, she knew what questions to ask. And knowing what was going on in class made it easier to understand the textbooks. The two aspects of school sort of fed on each other.

As she slowly became a student, she thought, sometimes, that she could even understand things that her teachers didn't. But she didn't challenge them, yet. She was destined to become a real nuisance in high school, but not yet.

And then she learned some test tricks. Like, if she not only *understood* the different kinds of algebra problems, but actually *drilled* on them, she could get really fast at solving them, and ace the timed tests. Then she discovered that doing that was more than a test trick. She was transforming her mind. She was beginning to think in numbers and their patterns. She was becoming a mathematician.

Something similar was happening in her history class. At first she assumed that memorizing the presidents' names and dates was a silly waste of time, and she agreed with her classmates that it was really a torture devised by the teacher because he was a sadist. April simply wouldn't have done it had she not already decided to for other reasons. After all, unless her grades improved, her mother would have won her secret case against studying—the case underlying her stated case *for* studying.

It was the end of the school year before she started to realize what she was actually doing with her history memorizing. The dates, and presidencies, had started taking on personalities, depending on what was going on at that time in history. It felt sort of like the personalities that playing cards developed when she used to play blackjack a lot with Ned and Robbie and Angie, so that she could remember which cards had been played in any deal. Or the suits in bridge, although April hadn't got very far into bridge before it was trumped by swimming and study. Much to her mother's disappointment.

Finally she was able to build a whole sort of shelving system of the personalities of the different historical times, that she could stick events or people into to give them contexts. She started with the obvious ones—Washington and the revolution, Lincoln and the civil war, TR and the bully turn-of-the-century times, with young Alice Roosevelt, who could have been her heroine if she hadn't been so blue-eyed and popular—but she soon added the personalities of the other eras. Later she decided she preferred decade personalities, like the "Roaring Twenties," to presidential personalities.

Within a semester the initial damage had been done. She was a student, and Mother was the one who had to retreat. When she looked at April's report card, she shook her head. "Well," she said, "you're not like me. You're not even like your brother. I don't know *who* you're like. But you seem to know what you're doing. I sure don't, but I can't really complain."

However, it was something that happened the summer before April entered high school that finally turned her mother from resistance to acceptance, and even support, if not the kind April might have wanted.

April had a summertime problem. The only school pool in the system was at her junior high, and it would be closed the first half of the vacation. Her teammates welcomed the break, but April simply couldn't imagine taking that much time off from her workouts.

There had been talk of installing a pool at the high school, but then the possibility of building a whole new high school came up, so everything was postponed until decisions were made. Vesey pool was crowded with splashing kids all summer long. There were two other pools in the area, one at the "Y" and the other at the country club, but both required memberships. April was sure her mother wouldn't buy her a "Y" membership just so she could work out.

Still, she was building up the courage to ask, when Marcia called her and invited her to visit the country club pool as her guest. April thought, "Why not?" and accepted. Her mother would have to take her, but she thought she would.

But when she asked, Mother became strangely ill at ease. "Well, Hon, I'm not sure that would be . . . Marcia's parents would be charged, you know. They charge for guests at those places."

"Well, she invited me," said April.

"I know, Honey. I just don't . . . I mean, you know how you are."

"How I am?"

"I mean, one swim wouldn't be enough for you, would it?" She thought for a moment, then she asked, "What's Marcia's last name?"

"Martindale."

"Oh," said Mother. "Oh, I see. Umm . . . do you know if her mother's name is Marilyn?"

April had met Marcia's mother briefly, but she didn't know her first name.

"Well . . . let me think about it, Honey. Not for long, I promise. I'll decide this afternoon, so you can tell Marcia."

And April had to go read while she waited. It occurred to her that she could take the bus. She didn't have to depend on her mother to give her a ride. It would be the first time she'd actually gone against her mother's wishes about something involving other people, and she felt uneasy about it. But she was getting angry.

92

She heard Mother make a couple of telephone calls, but didn't listen. But then she heard her call up the stairs. "April? Hon, Marcia's mother is Marilyn Martindale. I'm going to give her a ring."

"Who?" asked April, jumping out of bed.

"Marilyn Martindale. I met her . . . oh, I don't know, a while back. I just thought I'd tell you first."

"Mother, I . . ."

"Don't worry, Hon. I'm not trying to interfere with your plans. I think I can help you with this."

In spite of herself, April managed to hold her temper. What her mother just said was nonsense, but odd enough that it de-fused her growing emotion. But she did tiptoe to the top of the stairs to listen to the call.

She heard her introduce herself as April's mother. Marcia's friend, April. Apparently Marilyn Martindale knew who she was. "Yes, they seem to be very close," said Mother. "Yes, thanks very much. That was very kind of you . . . Yes, she'd love to come. But actually, I'm calling about something slightly different—I mean related, but different. I've been thinking for a long time of applying for membership at Brentwood, myself. . . . Oh, yes, I enjoy the occasional round of golf, or tennis . . ."

April made her wry face, in spite of her amazement at what her mother was saying.

"Bridge! Oh, yes, very much. I'm a little rusty now, but . . . Pardon? . . . Oh, you mean Ned? Yes, we're very proud of him .

. . yes, a family membership. I would want them both to be included. Yes. Anyway, Marcia inviting April to come as her—I mean, your guest—made me realize that now would be a good time , , , Yes, real estate. Yes, my own business—for better or worse!"

Marilyn Martindale must have been a big talker, because they went on and on. Finally she heard Mother calling her. "April? Come down! I have something very exciting to tell you!"

"Well," Mother began, when April stumbled down the steps. Mother had her beaming smile on, standing with her feet apart in her exultation posture, with her hands on her hips. She normally stood like that only when she'd made a big closing. "I've been invited too!"

"Invited? To swim?"

"No, Silly. For lunch. You and Marcia will swim in the morning—she says that's the time for lap swimming—and then you'll fix yourselves up and meet us for lunch. I'll take you there at ten, and then, while you're swimming, I've been invited to tour the premises! *And* attend to my application—to Brentwood Country Club! You'll be able to swim any time! Any time they'll let you, of course. Then lunch! With Marilyn Martindale! You know, she's George Martindale's wife. Isn't it exciting?"

April was open-mouthed, but she nodded. In fact, she'd never heard of either of them in that way, although she knew one of them was Marcia's mother. And she wasn't sure about excitement, either. She hadn't expected her mother to get this close to her training routines. She still hadn't figured out what it all meant.

94

"Mother, isn't that . . . isn't it very expensive? A membership?"

"Outrageous," Mother said. "I may be just kidding myself about how fast the payback will come. But that's not my main reason. See, Honey, I've been working very hard, for years. Raising you kids and growing the business. My only social life has been through my work, with my clients. They come and go, you know. And of course, Jan and Clark." They were her employees, sort of—her agents—whom April saw from time to time, when she stopped by the office. "And, I just think it's time . . . I don't just want a break, like a vacation. I want a change of lifestyle.

"And I've been thinking about this. I'd have done it by now, but . . .well, see, I didn't know anybody. There, at Brentwood, I mean. I've done business with some of them, of course. But never made close friends with anyone. Which is really what you need. They have to vote you in, you know. And it's still very hard for divorced women to be invited. There are several single female members, but they all started out with their husbands. Only one or two divorcees have been invited to join.

"But . . . see, Honey, *you do* know somebody there! And I realized . . . Marilyn will want to help her daughter, just as I want to help you! And she seemed very pleased to get the star quarterback in on the deal! So, I'll help you with your swimming, but you're helping me too! To get what I've wanted for a long time. See?"

April wasn't sure she could see, but she nodded again. There was no doubt Mother had worked hard, and April knew about

95

the sacrifices she'd made for her and Ned, although she'd only recently started seeing it that way. And she couldn't remember her mother talking to her so much, all at once, ever before. She was impressed by that. Not to mention by the sudden solution to her pool problem.

"So, Hon, do we have a deal?"

Now April was puzzled again. "A deal?"

"Yes. You know, as I've told you, that I know we've gone off on different tracks, you and I. I don't know where you're going, as I said, but I trust you to find your own way. And I'll help you as much as I can. But I need you to help me, too. Will you do that?"

It didn't occur to April that she was asking for something specific. "Sure," she said. "I appreciate you helping me to swim, and I'll help you if I can."

"Oh, good, Honey. I'm so pleased. I just have one big favor to ask. I think Brentwood will be very good for you. If we get in, that is. You'll make lots of good friends there. But I just want . . . as a favor to me—a return favor—please, please, do your best to look as nice as you can when you're there."

Mother must have seen the change of expression on April's face, because her voice became pleading. "Is that too much to ask? Please, I understand your reasons. I think I do. But can't you just give me that much? You must be over your rebellion, or whatever it was, by now. Enough to do your mother a favor. Just do what Marcia does. She knows how to do it, I'm sure. Just watch her, and do the same thing. It just won't work, unless you do. Please, for me?"

The idea of just imitating her friend appealed to April far more than having to figure out how to "look nice" on her own. And as she thought about it, she knew that not caring how she looked hadn't been a rebellion. She'd just given up hope, at first, then she'd decided that was part of the new April. But if her mother would accept her efforts, she could try to look nice for her, if for nobody else. Why not? "Mother," she finally said, "I'm not going to spend a lot of time on my face. But the rest of it, I'll try."

"Oh, Honey, that's *wonderful!*" Said Mother, and she came over to give her a hug. April returned her hug, and shared her mother's feeling of relief. Then Mother backed off a few steps, and looked at her, her head cocked to the side, as though she were assessing a problem. "Now, let's see," she said. "You'll need some new summer clothes."

April's mother seemed very happy at the outcome of their long conversation, but there were many things about it that April didn't understand. Because it had been very strange.

Mother had never before talked about herself like that. This time she talked about her own needs and wants, and admitted that April could help her. Help *Mother*! It had always worked the other way around. No . . . not exactly. Before, it had always been *us*. What her mother had decided to do to help the family, all *three* of us.

Now she was talking about herself as a separate person. And April was a separate person too. Because she'd chosen to be. And that's why they had to do a *deal.* Like what mother did with other separate people when she sold them houses. A contract.

It was slowly becoming clear that Mother was asking her to give up what she took to be the rebellious teenager pose. She would let her be who she wanted to be, and *in return* she expected her daughter to . . . not to harm her social and business standing, by dressing wrong. A deal.

April had a mixture of feelings about all that. She was pleased and flattered that her mother was treating her with what she must have thought of as respect, and very pleased that she was letting her go her own way. Still, while she recognized all that, she had the uneasy suspicion that Mother had defined their contract so that she was getting her own way after all. That April might find her freedom curtailed again.

But as she considered her new independence, she suddenly felt something else. Only in passing. A little chill of uncertainty. And loneliness.

*   4   *

As it turned out, however, that summer before high school was to be memorable for April, and transformational, in several unexpected ways.

Her first workout with Marcia felt different, as she might have expected, since they were on their own for the first time. The pool was impressive. It was new, and the full fifty meters long, if only six lanes wide and less than four feet deep, getting gradually a little deeper at the near end, April guessed for diving starts. Marcia said there were plans to host some meets.

There were other lap swimmers in the pool with them but most of the other people were older. It occurred to her that the old folks might be the reason for the shallow pool. April didn't know any of them, although she'd seen the boy lifeguard before. He was on the high school swimming team.

April and Marcia had to share a lane, which they were used to doing. They swam their laps as usual, starting with the crawl, slowly, then faster and faster according to their well-practiced warmup plan, keeping to the right at mid-pool to avoid collisions and doing their well-practiced flip turns at the ends. Then after their dozen laps they took a breather, and then started with their own strokes, April with the butterfly, and Marcia with her backstroke. Fifty meters at a time, with a timed break after each lap. There was a big clock on the wall, with a big sweep-second hand, for timing.

After a while they saw they'd collected some viewers, standing and talking to the lifeguard and watching them. When they finished their workout and climbed out of the pool, they got a little round of applause. April realized that their workout must be unusual for that pool, especially since they had it down to a routine.

The showers were little individual stalls, with little individual shower-stall-size dressing rooms in front of each, where they'd hung their clothes. The mirrors and so on for finishing up were out in the main locker room. As they went into their stalls, Marcia said, "Want to share a shower with me too?" April laughed. But she would think about it later.

Their first Brentwood workout, and the lunch gathering afterward, had been postponed to Saturday, to give April's mother a chance to take her shopping for her "summer clothes" the day before. Mother had mentioned that Ned might come along for the lunch, but he hadn't arrived when she dropped April off earlier.

There was a bit of a kerfuffle about what to wear after the swim. Mother had got April some fitted jeans, which she said looked nice. But she'd also got her some pretty summer dresses made of a light crinkly material that could be bundled up and stuck in a sports bag. April had worn her new jeans, but she'd brought along a pretty dress, because Mother had told her to wear it to lunch. She put it on.

But when Marcia saw her she looked horrified. "No!" she said, her hands to her cheeks. "No, you mustn't!"

April was genuinely startled. Marcia had never said anything like that to her. "Mustn't what?" she managed to say.

Marcia immediately responded to the look on April's face. "Oh, no, I didn't mean it," she said. "I mean . . . I do mean it, but not that way." She came up to her and took her by the shoulders.

"I'm so sorry. I didn't mean . . .to surprise you." Then she hugged her. It was the first time she'd done that.

"Mother said I should . . ."

"Oh, yes, it's very pretty," said Marcia. "Mothers say things like that. But don't you see? If you wear a dress, I'll have to wear one too." April saw Marcia had her usual jeans on. "Come on, April. Let's dress like we want to. I know you get that. We're teenagers! Please, for me. You came in jeans, right?"

April just stood there for a moment, stunned. She realized that she felt far more shocked, and even hurt, than the occasion called for. Finally, she went again into the stall and changed back into her fitted jeans and camisole and white blouse.

"I'm so sorry, April," said Marcia. "I shouldn't have reacted so strongly. But really! That could get us both into terrible trouble."

April's laugh was a little forced, but she guessed she pulled it off. "I see that now!" she said.

Later she would think what an awful spiral of doubt and destruction Marcia's immediate apology had snatched her back from. When she went back in her booth to change again, she was actually thinking: any place that takes clothes this seriously isn't for me. She could have walked out right then, and almost did. It took her a lot more thinking, later, to figure out that Marcia felt something like the same way as she did. It was the mothers who took the clothes seriously. And April and Marcia had to stand together against them. And April could see that the way Marcia

101

was doing it was close to the way she herself was trying to work it out with her own mother. Less trouble that way. And she didn't really want to hurt Mother's feelings.

For the moment, she just hoped Mother would understand that she hadn't broken their contract. Hadn't she told her to imitate Marcia?

As they walked to the clubhouse, where the dining room was, April realized she was still disturbed by something. Marcia was going on about how their jeans were fine for a Saturday anyway, and April saw that her disturbance was caused by the fact that neither Marcia nor she had really escaped taking clothes seriously. She'd realized that before, thinking of the elaborate dress the "punks," and new "gothics," and other kids at school came up with in order not to be normal. April had been forced to respond, after all, to two very serious, and even urgent solicitations in a single week, from two people who were important to her, that she dress the way they wanted her to!

They walked into the dining room, April carrying her new sports bag. The room was quite large, and while it was a little rustic, it had deep carpeting and big chandeliers hanging from the ceiling beams. It was full of people for Saturday lunch. April looked around for a little table with their two mothers. She didn't see them.

"C'mon," said Marcia. "There they are, over at our table." As they walked toward the big windows overlooking the golf course, April saw two men stand up at the big round table in the corner, and then a third. She recognized the late stander as Ned.

"Well, here are the mermaids!" said the older man with a smile. "Kindly join us."

"Hi Dex," said Marcia, walking over to the tall young man. "April, this is Dexter, my boyfriend. And you know my mother. And this is my Dad, George Martindale." April was nodding and smiling, and she walked around and stuck out her hand to shake Mr. Martindale's. She didn't say anything, but everyone was smiling so she hoped that was okay.

"I'm Ned," said Ned.

"Who?" said April.

They all sat.

"Good swim, Hon?" said her mother.

"Great," said April. "Nice pool."

"Yes, we're very pleased with it," said Marcia's mother. "It's very popular. It's new, you know."

"So Marcia was telling me," said April.

As the casual conversation continued, April looked at her mother for the first time. She was smiling her genuine smile, so April knew her clothing decision was okay. In fact, most of the people in the room were in sporting clothes of some kind—golfing gear, mostly. A couple of women were even wearing tennis shorts. The only person anything like dressed up was George Martindale. He had on slacks and a sports coat, with an open shirt. Nobody else had jackets except Ned, who was dressed like George Martindale, and April had never seen his sports coat before. Mother's doing. Dexter was in pressed trousers and a starched shirt.

Mother was dressed in her usual nice way. So was Marcia's mother. April noticed for the first time that she was strikingly beautiful, even though she was Mother's age. Marcia's dad seemed to be older.

The interrupted conversations continued now. George seemed mainly interested in talking to Ned. He was telling him about sports at his old alma mater, and April could overhear things like, "the best-funded athletic program in the state, and if I say so, the best supported by the alums," and, "as I'm sure you know, next year, your senior year, you're going to have so many people wanting to talk to you, you'll be wishing you never played the game," to which Ned answered, "Oh, I doubt that, Sir." Ned seemed to be doing quite well. He'd obviously been well-coached. Mother was listening, while Marilyn Martindale pointed out various people in the room, saying things like, "Oh, there's Margie. Margie Cooper— you know, the law firm. You'll definitely want to meet her." Mother was nodding her agreement.

April got the impression that Mother was moving ahead with her application. She seemed to fit right in.

April herself had no apparently assigned conversation partner, and that suited her. She hoped her smiles signaled she was content. What puzzled her was what Marcia was doing. She was sitting by Dexter, and saying a few things to him, and touching him from time to time, as girls tend to do to their boyfriends—although they're usually a little older when they do it, April thought—and

Dexter was enjoying the attention, as boys also tend to do.

But the puzzling thing was that almost all of Marcia's actual attention was being directed to her. To April. With looks, and little gestures, like rolling her eyes at the slightest uncool thing some of the older folks said. Or just long gazes, while Dexter or someone else was talking to her, directing her attention at them just for a quick reply. And then back to April.

April felt she knew Marcia. She'd seen her nearly every day for a whole semester, and spent hours with her most of those days. As the only junior high kids on the high school team, they naturally stayed together. But they'd never been "close," as April had been with Angie. They hadn't shared secrets or forbidden opinions. April knew nearly nothing about Marcia's life away from school. She'd never even heard about Dexter!

Marcia now seemed to be trying very hard to get closer to April. April liked the attention, as Dexter did, but didn't understand it.

Quite a few people visited their table. Several men wanted to meet Ned, and tell him what positions they'd played on the high school team, and reminisce about their own days there. One of them asked Dexter how his golf game was going. Apparently that was Dexter's thing. "Down to nine," Dexter answered, and the man said "Whoa," and looked impressed. Dexter's parents came over to say hello to Marcia and greet her parents, and find out when he would be home.

And a couple of people who'd seen the girls swimming walked over and commented on it. "You girls are something else," one little pudgy man said. "I mean, *fast.* And you just keep going and going, like that bunny rabbit. You know," he continued, looking at April, "I used to do some swimming, and I tried that butterfly. That's *hard!* You made it look like you were born doing it. Do you girls have fins?"

The girls smiled, and when their fan started talking to George, Marsha glanced at the ceiling, in another mini-eye-roll, and flashed her smile at April. April noticed it was almost identical to Marilyn's smile.

Ned took an interest in the man's comments too, and gave April a questioning expression. She realized he hadn't seen her swim since she'd started her workouts. And then George asked, "April, have you heard of Title Nine?"

"No, Sir," she said.

"Ah, you and I need to talk too," said George.

April nodded, and smiled at that also, since smiles and nods had got her by so far. Then she looked at Mother. Mother raised her eyebrows and nodded slightly at her, in a "that sounds promising" gesture. April guessed that Mother didn't know what Title Nine was either, but if it reinforced her approval of her swimming, April was all for it.

As they all walked out to their cars, April asked Marcia, in a whisper, "So, did I do okay?"

"Wonderful!" Said Marcia. "Your Mother won't have any complaints. Or shouldn't."

"I doubt I said three words the whole time."

"No, no. That's just you. You're not exactly a big talker, are you? You responded to everybody. Without words. You were lovely!" And Marcia put her arm around her as they walked, and gave her a little squeeze.

April felt she was seeing a new Marcia, and realized that this was the first time she'd been with her on Marcia's home turf, and exactly how at home she was here. In the school workouts, April had always felt that Marcia was sort of following her lead, and had got used to making decisions for them both. Here, it was April who felt unsure, and Marcia who was taking the lead.

After that day, Mother couldn't contain her new enthusiasm for April's chosen sport. What did she need? A new swimming suit? Of course she did. Marcia had a black one, made of some material that was supposed to reduce friction in the water, and Mother insisted that April have one too, and also several pairs of shorts and pretty blouses to wear to and from her workouts. Mother was in her element. April had never seen her so happy.

What April really needed was a way to get to the Club (as Mother called it), and back, every day. No problem. Mother could take her some days, and Ned was drafted for the other times. The most exciting thing about that was that Ned would stay, sometimes with Helen, and watch April and Marcia go through their routine. He acted impressed with his little sister. And he also acted like he enjoyed talking to the old guys who always wanted to chat about football and old times.

The meeting to vote on new members at the Club wouldn't be until September, but Marilyn said that was a good thing, since it gave her time to "line things up." Marilyn also accepted Mother's offer to pay the charges for April's use of the pool, after some, "Oh, no, don't be silly! You don't have to worry about that," and "Oh, really, I insist." Mother said Marilyn's acceptance was also a good thing, because it meant that she "considers us equals."

After a while, Ned got tired of giving April rides, and of the football conversations, and besides, Fall practice would start in a few weeks. April sympathized. But she had a solution, and she and Ned agreed that there was no need to involve Mother until the big change was accomplished. After workouts, they would check out cycling shops, although they had no intention of buying new. They asked a lot of questions, mainly about types of bicycles, and tire sizes and pressures, and got a feeling for frame brands and metals and gear systems and brakes.

Then April watched the ads in the paper, and finally saw a bike she could afford, an ordinary road model with three hub gears. Fortunately she had nowhere else to spend her allowance, and so had saved most of it. Ned took her to get it, and she was riding it in front of the house, with Ned and Helen laughing and shouting advice, when Mother came home from work.

She parked the car in the drive, and walked out to the curb. She looked puzzled. "April?" she said, as April rode by and waved. She watched April riding around for about a minute, ignoring the greetings and comments from the other watchers. "Is that yours, Helen?" April heard her ask.

"No, ma'am," Helen answered.

"All right, then. Ned, where did she get it?"

"She bought it," said Ned.

By this time April had stopped and hopped off the seat, and was standing astraddle her new bike, a big grin on her face. "I got it cheap," she said. "With my allowance money."

"Well . . . but Honey, when will you play with it? You know how busy you are."

Ned assumed the duty of explaining. "It's to get to the Club. You know, football's starting in a couple of weeks, and . . ."

"The Club? Ride a *bicycle* to the *Club?* No. No, absolutely not." Mother turned, and took a few assertive steps toward the house. But then she stopped, turned around, and took some equally assertive steps back. April could tell she was upset, but about what she had no idea. "You can't . . . Honey, what about your *promise?* You *promised* me, remember?"

"Promised you?"

"Yes! You promised me you'd . . . do things right. At the Club."

"You mean . . . wear my pretty clothes?"

"Yes, your pretty clothes. When that's what other people are wearing. But other things—whatever *everybody does.* At the Club. Do you *ever* see people on bicycles there?"

April couldn't remember whether she'd ever seen people on bicycles at the Club or not.

"I'm sorry, April. You should have asked! I know football's about to start, Ned. In three weeks. But can't you take just a *little* break from swimming, April? Before school starts? Everybody else does. Your *whole team* has been on break *all summer*! Anyway, you can't ride that thing on the streets. It's dangerous! These people around here drive like crazy!"

"The roads aren't busy until just before you get there," said Ned in a loud voice. "And she can ride on the sidewalks. Nobody cares. You know Mark Becker? Our defensive linebacker? He rides a bike to school every day. For the extra workout. Everybody knows that's why he does it. Hell, I was thinking I'd start doing it myself!"

"You have your car, Ned. I don't want to have to worry about either of my children, out on the roads, unprotected. You know people don't notice bicycles in this town. Anyway, this is between me and your sister."

Helen was staring wide-eyed. Ned grabbed her hand, and pulled her to his car, parked by the curb. They got in and left.

"I don't . . ." April started. But she didn't know what to say. Or what to think.

"Put that thing in the garage. Give me a chance to calm down. I'm sorry, April, but sometimes you're just impossible. We'll talk about it later." And she went in.

April got off her bicycle and walked it around back. The garage door was closed, so she just stood it by the drive. She looked at it, thinking how happy it had made her just a few minutes before, and how she'd got it all wrong. Then she walked behind the garage and sat, her back leaning against the wall. She was shaken. But after a while, she was just unhappy. She didn't even consider anger. She was too confused for that.

Like her mother, she thought they had an agreement. And she thought she'd been keeping her side of it. She thought Mother was pleased with her. Now she felt she could never be sure.

Mother did come to April's room later, and apologized in a way. "You know how important this whole thing is to me," she said. "I think it's going okay, but sometimes . . . I just get a little on edge. You do understand, don't you?"

"Yes ma'am," said April.

*   5   *

As April was waking up the next morning, and her heavy memories of the day before clicked into place one by one, she found their weight still holding her spirits down. She'd thought about it as she went to sleep the night before, and decided it had just been an innocent mistake on her part. She just didn't know about the prohibition against bicycles. And her mother knew she didn't, really. She'd all but said so.

And likewise, April understood her mother's anxiety about fitting in at the Club. It was something like a big math test Mother and her family were taking, an equation they were working out, where every step in the solution covered up a possible deadly mistake. Like picking their way across a field where there was a scorpion under every leaf. But that was what was oppressing April. How could she be sure the day wasn't readying another big hidden trap for her to stumble into? And when her mother became a member of the Club, could they relax then? Or would they always have to worry about getting it right?

It was all she could do to go through her routine of getting ready for her morning workout. As for that thing in the garage—if anybody had put it in—she hated it.

Marcia noticed that April was "a little down," and April told her what had happened. She suspected that she shouldn't tell her, but she couldn't help it. Marcia just shook her head, whether in sympathy, or surprise, or a vague refusal to accept, April couldn't tell.

But she soon found out.

Taking April to the Club for her workout the following morning, Mother stopped the car at the little guardhouse to sign in, as they still had to do until they were members. While they were waiting, Marcia rode by in the members' lane. On a bicycle. A pretty blue one. She grinned and waved.

April and Mother looked at each other. They were equally dumbfounded.

112

After a silence, Mother said, "I suspect a plot."

"I . . . I don't know," said April. "I didn't plot anything."

"But you told her."

"I . . . yes. I told her you didn't want me riding a bike. For transportation. I said you thought it was dangerous."

"Yes, and I still do," said Mother.

And that's all that was said, as Mother let her out. April smiled and waved bye-bye.

She was experiencing a very strong feeling as she walked up to the gym door, where Marcia was waiting—a mixture of wonder that Marcia would have thought of it, and gone to the trouble, and also of gratitude, even though she suspected that it wouldn't do any good. And a kind of self-reassurance, as though she'd been propped up. Which, she felt, was exactly what Marcia had done. And that was what she was most grateful for.

Marcia had also propped her bike up, near the door, on its stand. "I don't think I need to chain it or anything," she said.

April walked straight up to Marcia and hugged her. For a long time. "Thanks, Marcia," she said.

"Any time," said Marcia, giving April a little squeeze in return. "We need to take care of each other."

Take care of each other. April knew that. But she'd never actually thought it.

As they were cutting through the "sports arena," the Club's sort of half-gym, on their way to the locker rooms, April was feeling a huge sense of release, of jubilation. She felt like dancing and

113

whirling around. She did it, a little. Then she noticed the big wrestling mat they were walking by, on the floor at the near end of the arena. It wasn't actually used for wrestling—nobody at the Club wrestled—but it was kept out, mainly as a safe area for little kids to fall about on so their mothers could watch them while doing their treadmill trots or light weights in the glass-walled exercise room next door. There was nobody there now.

"Want to wrestle?" April asked. She pulled Marcia out onto the mat, and took a half-crouch stance which she made up on the spot. Marcia just stood there looking quizzically at her. But when April made a kind of fake charge at her, she found herself seized in a surprisingly strong grip, and the next thing she knew she was on her back on the mat, with Marcia holding her down and grinning at her. Marcia had somehow picked her up and laid her down before she knew what was happening.

"Didn't you say you wanted to wrestle?" said Marcia.

April took a few breaths before answering, "Let's do that again." Marcia was bigger than she was, but she had no idea that she was that strong. Although she should have guessed—Marcia kept up with April in their workouts. Now she knew. And it felt familiar. It brought back her years of roughhousing with Ned, who was, of course, also much stronger than she was.

They got up and faced each other again. April got close enough for Marcia to make another grab at her, but this time she jumped back. Then she got close again, but when Marcia lunged,

April sidestepped, grabbed her arm, and pulled in the direction

114

of her lunge. Marcia reacted by pulling back, and April then stepped behind her, and used Marcia's backwards momentum to trip her over her hip and outstretched leg onto her back on the mat. Marcia tried to sit up, but April quickly fell on top of her and pushed her back down, holding her wrists to the mat with her hands.

And as she did that, April's eyes glanced down at Marcia's chest. It was only a glance. Marcia's big breasts had heaved up, under her shirt, when her back hit the mat with April on top. And April noticed the motion, and glanced down at them before she could stop herself. Immediately she looked back in Marcia's eyes, and said what she'd planned to say if she managed to pin her: "Yes, I said I wanted to wrestle." But it didn't have the note of triumph she'd intended. The mood had changed.

Marcia gave a little smile, and then did something strange. She closed her eyes.

April stared at her, waiting for her to open them. But she kept them closed.

April realized Marcia had seen her looking. But she didn't understand what Marcia was doing now. Finally April got up, and with a big fake sigh, intended to disguise her genuine confusion, she walked over and sat on the second bench of the little bleacher on the nearby wall.

Marcia lay there on her back for another minute, then she opened her eyes, got up and came over and sat, sort of facing April, on the bottom bench.

She was staring down. "April, I thought . . . see, I thought maybe you wanted to . . . to look at me."

April didn't know what to say. She didn't want to look at Marcia. Actually, she'd had the occasional flash of curiosity. Wondering what they looked like, and assuming that she had some sort of right to know. She couldn't see anything like that in the mirror. But she didn't want actually to look.

She realized, then, that Marcia must have misinterpreted the whole sequence—the invitation to wrestle—maybe even the long hug she'd given her to show her appreciation. And because she'd felt like hugging her.

"See . . ." Marcia started, but stopped, and didn't say anything else for a while. April didn't either.

"April, I want . . . we need to be close to each other. I don't want to have any secrets. I want us to . . . to feel comfortable. We should feel comfortable looking at each other."

No! something inside April said. No. Maybe April looking at Marcia. Maybe just that. Marcia was a normal girl. Young woman. Boys looked at each other all the time. They got naked and showered together. They got used to it. But April knew she wouldn't feel comfortable with Marcia looking at her. So the whole deal was off.

And then, out of nowhere, she found herself saying what she felt. Her mouth opened, and the words came out: "I don't want you to look at me."

But then Marcia did look up at her. She didn't say anything for a moment—she seemed to be absorbing April's words. Then she said, "But April, you're beautiful!"

"Oh, no," said April. "No. I know I'm not. That's not what I meant. I don't know why you said that. I don't need you to say that. I know better, and I don't care."

Marcia looked genuinely incredulous. And as April looked at her face, she saw that it was wet. Marcia had been crying! Quietly.

April really didn't understand what was going on.

"You are!" said Marcia. "You're beautiful! You're . . . you're fierce!"

"I'm what?" said April. "I'm *what?*" And then, in spite of herself, she started giggling.

And Marcia did too. Then they were both giggling and crying at the same time. And then they were standing, and hugging each other again, as the little children came out, a little girl and a little boy.

"Oh, is it all right?" said their mother, following behind them. "If they play here while I'm on the treadmill? Will they be in your way?"

"No, no, of course not," said Marcia. "We're just leaving."

And they continued their trek toward the locker rooms, still giggling. April felt relieved. The situation between them seemed to return to where it had been before the wrestling match. They were acting relaxed with each other, like they were trying to reassure each other that it was all okay. For the first time, before the wrestling, April had been feeling as close to Marcia as she used to feel with Angie, and it felt familiar and good. She didn't really like being so alone. She'd just thought it was necessary. And now she didn't want to let the closeness go, because of some sort of odd misunderstanding.

But she was still amazed—puzzled and a little frightened—at the strange tension between them that had made them cry. And giggle, out of nowhere. And that had just happened, just then.

April took refuge in their now familiar workout routine, and found herself sharing more than the usual allotment of smiles and little laughs and touches with Marcia. They enabled April to put her own mind at ease, and her partner's, while keeping her distance until she could get a more secure understanding of what was going on between them. Or get over it. Whatever it was.

That was on a Friday, and was followed by a weekend featuring, for April, some emotional turmoil. They hadn't swum on Saturdays after that first visit to the Club pool, because weekends were Marcia's time for family and Dexter. It would have been family time for April too, except that Saturdays, and sometimes Sunday afternoons, were Mother's busiest time for showing houses, and Ned spent most of the weekend with Helen. Sometimes Ned would ask April to go to a movie with them, but April always refused.

So she sprawled on the couch in the living room, and continued with the book she was reading. But she wasn't paying much attention. She'd realize she was just staring at the pages, or that she'd read a whole page without taking in a word of it. Then her discipline would kick in, and she'd make herself forget her worries, or whatever they were, and would manage to get through another page or two before they returned.

After their incident in the sports arena, for the couple of hours she and Marcia were together, smiles and touches had been enough. She didn't have to think about it. But now that she was by herself, apparently she did.

So, she decided she'd just try to think about it. She lay on her back with her book on her tummy and her eyes closed, and waited for her feelings to explain themselves to her.

Somebody had told her, once—or maybe she'd just heard it on the radio, or the TV, before Mother made her stop watching it because she and Angie "never did anything else"—somebody had said that the way to do it was "feel out the sore places." April had decided that what that meant was to think about it until she could feel what was bothering her most.

So she did. She went back through what had happened, and what she and Marsha said to each other. She'd been doing that all morning, of course, but this time she paid more attention to how she'd felt about it at the time. Everything had been all right—especially all right, April was feeling, because of Marcia's trick with the bicycle—until the business about looking at Marcia came up. But why?

Did she think it was *wrong*? Maybe deep inside? But even as the idea occurred to her, April knew it couldn't be that. That idea felt alien. It was somebody else's idea, not hers. April had gone to church, for several years in fact. Mother used to take them both, April and Ned, when they were kids, and leave them in Sunday School while she attended the service. They both hated it. It was boring. Ned finally threw such a fit that Mother gave up the whole project.

Later April had gone to a different church with Angie and her family. Mother had seemed pleased that Angie had invited April, but she hadn't gone herself, using her Sunday house-showings as an excuse, or a reason. In fact, April came to realize, Mother attended church mainly for the business contacts, and because she thought it would be good for the kids. But when she got the chance to skip it herself, she'd taken advantage of it. She'd sort of "sent" April to church.

April guessed that her years attending two churches could have given her the feeling that what Marsha seemed to want from her was wrong. But she couldn't actually find that feeling inside her.

Yet she knew that most of the girls at school would feel uneasy about it, just as she did. Many of them had never seen the inside of a church. And yet again—the *boys,* she remembered

thinking, don't mind looking at each other. Why should girls?

120

Boys get naked and shower with each other, and think nothing of it. What's the difference?

What she really wanted to do was telephone Marcia. Discuss it with her. They often called each other on weekends, but it was always just to arrange something about their workouts. It wasn't like with Angie, when they would spend so long saying nothing on the phone, even though they lived only a few blocks from each other, that one of their mothers would finally end the conversation.

But something told April that she mustn't call Marcia. What would she say? "Marcia, what the hell is going on?" No. She had to wait until she'd figured it out for herself.

Maybe it was just that—just the fact that Marcia and she weren't really "best friends," as she and Angie had been. What were they, then? They spent as much time together as she and Angie ever had. But it was different. She and Marcia had a reason for the time they spent together, other than being friends. They were swimming buddies. They were . . . they were *teammates*. Teammates weren't supposed to look at each other, in that way. It just didn't fit.

Look at each other in what way?

But April scurried back from that question as quickly as she'd stumbled on it, and returned to her reading. Her alarm at the implications of the question blocked her from thinking about it further, for a good couple of hours. And by that time, preparations for her bike ride had begun.

"C'mon, April," Helen said. "Don't be lazy. We're going to Lake Wagner. C'mon."

"Oh, hi, Helen. I didn't hear you come in. Uh . . . no, thanks, I have a lot of stuff to do. Thanks anyway."

"No, you don't. What do you have to do? It's Summer. It's Saturday! C'mon, you have to come!"

April felt a little annoyed. Have to come? Of course she didn't *have* to come. What she did have to do was get her confusion sorted out. But then Ned was there too, and both of them were hauling her off the couch. "C'mon, Sis. Helen packed a lunch. We're going to have a picnic. After the ride. You don't want to miss it."

"What ride?" April couldn't help but ask. "Miss what?"

"We'll show you," said Ned, pulling her to her feet. "Outside."

April followed them out front. In the drive was a car, with some bicycles on top. April finally recognized the car as one she'd seen Helen driving before. She'd never seen the bicycles. They were standing up, held onto a rack by some straps. She now knew enough about bicycles that she could tell, by their skinny tires and the shape of their handlebars and all their gears, that they were fancy racers. And sticking out of the trunk, under a folded beach towel with the lid tied down onto it, was the front end of another bicycle. April had to stare for a moment before she recognized it as hers.

Suddenly she realized what Ned and Marsha were up to. And that they were doing it for her.

"I cleared it with Mother," said Ned, holding out a biker's helmet.

"Oh!" said April, clapping her hands with genuine pleasure. "Oh, let me go get some shoes on." She ran into the house, suddenly embracing this chance to escape her worries, in her excitement leaving Ned holding her helmet.

April learned on the way to the lake that the bikes on the rack above belonged to Helen's parents, who were, or used to be, keen cyclists, and that Lake Wagner had a tarmac cycling path entirely around its ten-mile circumference, separate from the hiking trails. When they arrived they were hungry, but they saw that there were a lot of people in the park, and that all the picnic tables were taken. So they decided to go ahead with their plan of riding first and picnicking afterwards. Helen said it would take about an hour.

April soon learned that, although she was as fit as either of the two older riders, their bicycles put them several classes above her when it came to speed. They were always having to stop and wait for her to catch up on her clunky old machine. Finally she told them she was having fun, which was true, and getting a good workout, and that she didn't need them to keep stopping. So they stopped less.

The lake was entirely surrounded by the park, which had big old trees in the full flourish of late summer, and warm breezes and smells. Sudden views of the lake through the trees, and long stretches of riding along its shore, and the unlooked-for appearance of flower gardens and blooming bushes kept things varied. April soon found she was absorbed by the surroundings, which seemed oddly familiar even though she'd never been here before, and even though what she was doing now was totally different from her daily reruns. By contrast, her workout routine suddenly seemed cold and harsh. It was as if she'd escaped from a stone prison in a foreign country, and found her way back home.

It began to dawn on her how rigid her life had become. She knew she'd chosen that way of life, and she wasn't going to change now. She had to do it, and she'd do it again. But . . . just a little relaxation . . .

"Left!" Another rider behind her shouted, coming around. That's what they did to warn her which side they were passing on. Course, it was always left, since she was sticking to the right.

Suddenly April found herself wondering if it were possible Marcia might be riding her blue bike here today. She really didn't know much about Marcia's weekends. For a while, she got lost in a little fantasy about meeting Marcia on the path, complete with the conversation they would have. Then it occurred to her that even if she did see Marcia, Dexter would be with her, so she'd have to wait until Monday to see her alone.

And until Monday suddenly seemed like an eternity.

How stupid, April thought, squelching the stupid feeling. She felt very uneasy about all these strange things going on inside her, that would pop up and take her by surprise. It was like part of her was rebelling against the rest of her. It didn't make sense. She'd already rebelled, against what Mother and all her former friends seemed to want her to be. Because she had to. She couldn't be those things. And she didn't want to be. But now she was rebelling against the rebellion!

And it all had to do with Marcia.

April shook her head abruptly, and stood up on the pedals and pumped hard to go faster. She had to get away from this somehow.

She concentrated on holding her new pace for a while. It was easier, now that she'd got the hang of the simple gearshift, but it took concentration. Particularly up the long slopes she wouldn't have noticed at all if she'd been walking or in a car.

She caught Ned and Helen around a curve. They hadn't stopped, they were just peddling slow and talking. "Left!" she shouted. Ned made some sarcastic comment, and moved ahead of Helen to let April by, and she pumped on past them. She thought Ned would chase her, which made her pump faster, even though she was already tired. The place where the car was parked was only a little way down the path, so it was like the final sprint in a distance race. But Ned wasn't chasing her.

What started bringing it all together for April was a single word Helen used while they were eating the cold fried chicken and potato salad that she'd made. She and Ned were talking about her, sort of making fun of her. "So, what do you think of my kid sister now?" Ned asked. "Maybe I'd better start thinking about moving over and letting her by."

"I'd say if you don't, your kid sister is about to give you some fierce competition," said Helen.

Fierce?

*   6   *

April woke up the next morning with her thighs sore from the ride. She was surprised: she hadn't realized before that putting your muscles through different movements than they were used to could give them the same symptoms as making them exercise for the first time.

But it told her that she'd had a workout—a totally different workout from her usual one, but still a real workout. And she felt she'd also had a real escape from what could become a killer routine. Her hour-long ride was so different that now it was as if she'd been on a vacation a thousand miles away. She still couldn't believe that Ned and Helen had come up with that. She felt everlastingly indebted to them. Maybe they'd saved her from going crazy.

She wanted more than anything to take that same ride with Marcia.

As she'd dozed off the night before, she'd seen a couple of things clearly. One was a distinction that Helen's use of the word "fierce" had made her think about. A distinction in her own mind, and a connection, that hadn't been there before. Marcia, when she'd used that word to describe April, had linked it with "beautiful." April didn't like to be called beautiful. She wasn't beautiful, and she didn't want to be judged by her looks anyway.

But Helen had connected her fierceness with her competitiveness. It had nothing to do with how she looked. And it occurred to April, in her ponderings, that Marcia must have meant something like the same thing. She'd said . . . she'd almost said . . . that April was beautiful *because* she was fierce. She had a beautiful *personality*, from Marcia's odd viewpoint. It just happened to come up in the context of looking at each other.

And that was the other thing she'd realized the night before. Boys don't get naked and shower together so that they can look at each other. They don't care what each other looks like. But Marcia *did* care. In fact, looking at each other was precisely what Marcia *wanted* to do. That was a big difference. And now that she realized that, April felt justified in refusing. If Marcia was going to like her, she'd have to do it without looking at her. She'd thought that whole business about looking at each other was crazy.

But as for fierceness—April kind of liked that idea. She could now see how Marcia might think of her that way. Compared to most people—even most of their teammates—April *was* "fiercely" *competitive*. And she remembered the screaming she'd done in the pool on that day she and Marcia first got together. That may have had nothing to do with competitiveness, but Marcia could have thought it did. Same as Coach Kemp.

April *wanted* to be competitive. And she didn't mind people thinking she was. And if Marcia wanted to think it was beautiful, she didn't mind that either.

But then . . . if Marcia didn't want to look at April because she was beautiful, why *did* she want to?

Well, maybe she didn't. She'd only thought April had wanted to look at *her*. And she was willing to look at April in return. Maybe to make it easier for April.

As Sunday dragged by, April lay in her bed with her book, and slowly sorted out the pieces of her puzzle, one piece at a time. She would see where one of the pieces fit when she didn't even know she was thinking about it. She would lay her book on her tummy and close her eyes and wait until the piece fitted itself into place.

It wasn't until late in the afternoon that she started to think how cold she'd been with Marcia. Once she saw that her refusal to let Marcia look at her had a lot more to do with her fears of being thought ugly than about any genuine principles of hers, she started contrasting that fearfulness with Marcia's desire for closeness. What right had April to deny Marcia her closeness, particularly after the very caring thing she'd just done for her, with the bicycle? Didn't April already know she looked ugly? And hadn't Marcia simply offered to accept her *as she was*?

And so, while April had worked out some of her thoughts and opinions about friends looking at each other, she ended her weekend still of two minds about what actually to do about it.

Finally, at some point, she dozed off, and was awakened by Mother, telling her the Sunday evening pizzas had arrived. She stretched, and shuffled sleepily into the kitchen to join Ned and Helen and Mother.

"Look what yesterday's easy ride did to our little athlete!" commented Ned. "I don't think I need to worry about any competition from her for a while."

After supper, April fetched her book again and went droopily up to bed, where, in spite of her nap, she soon fell asleep again, and slept soundly all night.

The next morning, everything seemed to have returned to normal again, and the emotional disturbances of the weekend looked silly. One thing she'd considered doing, half asleep the night before, was shave herself thoroughly just in case Marcia ended up looking at her, maybe by accident, sort of. Her arms and legs were already shaved well enough. She'd done it Friday morning, and her hair was light-colored. But there were parts of her that she'd never shaved—the areas covered by her swimming suit. Nobody ever saw those parts, so she didn't bother. She'd actually started planning how she'd go about it, before she fell asleep. She assumed her pubic hair was okay, since she'd never heard of anyone shaving that. But the rest of her tummy hair should go—if she could decide where one ended and the other began. And around her areolas.

Now, in the clear routine light of a Monday morning, that whole idea seemed ridiculous. If she was worried about that, she just wouldn't show herself. The chances of her doing so were nearly nil anyway.

Yet, even on a Monday morning, the thought flickered across her mind about how nice it would be if someone knew what she was really like, and accepted her anyway.

April took up with Marcia where she'd left off on Friday— full of smiles and good cheer. And more talkative than she usually was. She told Marcia all about the bicycle ride at Lake Wagner, and how good a workout it was, and what a good break, and how kind Ned had been, and that she was sure he could be talked into taking the two of them whenever they wanted to go.

Then April realized that she was doing all the talking. Marcia was different. She was aloof and unresponsive. She went about her preparations in silence.

"So, how was *your* weekend?" April asked.

"The usual," said Marcia, and disappeared into one of the dressing stalls.

April had wanted to tell her about her fantasy of seeing her on her bicycle at the lake, and about the conversation she'd imagined having with her. But the mood was certainly wrong for that. She couldn't tell if Marcia was just feeling down or if she was being sullen because of how April had acted the last time. Or because of something that had happened to her over the weekend. Or maybe she'd been doing some thinking of her own. April felt genuinely frightened of what she might have decided.

April changed into her bathing suit. When she came out of her stall, Marcia wasn't waiting, as they'd always done before.

April knocked on her stall door. "Marcia?" she said.

No answer. She walked into the pool area, and saw that Marcia was already starting her warmup. She got into the water, and waited for Marcia to reach the far turn before starting, to coordinate their laps as usual.

The same disagreeable spirit presided over the workout. April went out of her way to touch against Marcia when they passed each other, but Marcia didn't reciprocate. April thought that maybe Marcia would get out of the pool one lap early, when she was on the dressing room end, so she could get to her stall and get dressed and leave without any further dealings with April. She braced herself for it. But Marcia swam her final lap, as usual. So when April got out, she waited for Marcia to walk the length of the pool—the way they always did—so they could go into the dressing room together.

At that moment April decided what she had to do.

Neither girl said anything, but just as Marcia was about to go into her stall, April took her by the arm. "Marcia?" she said.

"What?" said Marcia.

"I want to shower with you," she said, letting go of her arm and stepping back. It wasn't easy to say that, but she was assisted by her need to get to the bottom of Marcia's sulkiness. She was ready to be rejected, if that's what was coming. Although she would hate it.

Marcia relaxed her posture, and stood with one knee forward as she did when she had to stand somewhere for a while. She looked at April a long time. It was a trying to decide look, April decided, and not a figuring out how to refuse look. Finally she said, "Are you sure? You'll have to look at me."

"I know," said April, smiling. She could feel herself blushing. She hadn't blushed in a long time.

"And I'll look at you," said Marcia.

April couldn't help covering her face with her hands. "I know," she said, between her palms.

But Marcia wasn't finished. When April lowered her hands, she was still looking at her, although April thought her look had softened a little.

"Why do you want to shower with me?" she asked.

Now April had to think. Finally she answered, "I want us to be close. I don't want us to have any secrets."

"And?" asked Marcia.

April thought some more. She couldn't think of anything else.

"What about taking care of each other?" said Marcia.

"I want us to take care of each other," responded April. "I mean, I want to take care of you, like you take care of me."

At that moment somebody came into the dressing room from outside. Marcia immediately opened the door to her stall, but muttered to April as she went in. "Come in when she's gone."

April smiled at the newcomer. "How's the water?" asked the lady.

"About right, if you keep moving," said April

"Oh," said the lady, "aren't you the new girl? The fast swimmer?"

"I'm . . . I'm trying to be fast," said April. "I'm April."

"April's always welcome," said the lady. "You're the friend of the Martindale girl, aren't you? Marcia."

"Yes Ma'am," said April.

"She's a fast swimmer too. Lovely young lady, Marcia," said the lady.

"Yes, she is," said April, although she wished it hadn't come up. She went into her stall, smiling. She took off her bathing suit, and wrapped her big towel around herself, not daring to look at her body. She sat down on the little bench under the clothes hooks, to wait.

She felt very nervous. But happier than she had been a few minutes ago.

After giving the lady time to change clothes and get to the pool, April peered out of her stall, and seeing nobody, she tiptoed to Marcia's stall, gave a quick rap on the door with her fingertip, and went in. She half expected to find Marcia gone.

But she wasn't gone. She was sitting on her bench, naked, leaning back into the corner, and gazing at April with the assertive sort of expression people use when they're trying to hide their actual uncertainty. Her lap was covered by a towel, but she threw it aside, as if to say, See? Total honesty. April smiled, to reassure her in case she needed it, and looked at her breasts.

They were bigger than she had imagined. Marcia had put her hands together on her lap, and that was enough to bring her breasts together with a crack between them. But then she placed her hands beside her, which allowed them to separate a little. April had imagined that they would stand out like cones, or something like that, but they were more like bags of water, with the nipples in a slightly different place than she had foreseen, pointing slightly upwards—not on the ends and pointing down. They looked stiff, like her own nipples got when they were cold, after a swim.

But the main impression her breasts gave was that they were full and imposing.

"So, that's what real ones look like," April said, and then giggled, a more nervous sound than she intended.

"Shhh," warned Marcia, glancing toward the door. "Do you think they're too big?" she whispered.

"Are you joking?" whispered April. "They're magnificent."

"They're already 'C's," said Marcia. "I'm only sixteen."

April felt a surge of the old inadequacy. Marcia had already outgrown two bra sizes, and April didn't even need a bra yet. She might never need one. "You're sixteen?" said April.

"Nearly. Not even sixteen. Think how big they'll be when I'm twenty-six!"

"I bet Dexter likes them," said April, still gazing.

Marcia made a shrugging, who cares face, and she also shrugged. Then, "Your turn," she said.

April suppressed an instinctive reaction, to pretend she didn't understand what she meant. She understood, all too well.

So, she closed her eyes, pulled the end of the towel loose, and let it drop to the floor. And she immediately covered her face again with her hands. That wasn't part of what she'd rehearsed, but she couldn't help it. She was terrified of seeing the expression on Marcia's face. She had noticed Marcia's little dark triangle between her legs, and knew that's what she was expecting.

There was a sort of gasp, and then a long silence. It went on forever. This is the end, April thought. She tried to think of something to say, something light-hearted and carefree. But then she realized Marcia was saying something. Sort of muttering.

"April, I had no idea . . ." she was saying. "I didn't know . . . I had no idea . . ."

She wasn't making sense. It made April hold her hands tighter over her face. It was scarcely a "fierce" gesture, but she didn't care. She just had to get through this.

Then she felt a touch on her tummy. Marcia was touching her tummy. With her knuckles, she could tell. She was stroking the hair on her tummy. It came as a surprise, and she may have jumped a little. But otherwise, she didn't move. She remembered her decision. And how much she had hated being separated from Marcia, just thirty minutes earlier. Although after this, they might be separated for ever.

Then she felt Marcia stand up—felt more than heard. She was standing right next to her. April could feel the heat from her body. Then Marcia took her by the shoulder and half turned her, half walked around her. She felt Marcia's stiff nipples brush against her arm. Now Marcia was standing behind her. Marcia took her arms and hugged her against her. April could feel Marcia's breasts pressing against her shoulder blades like a pillow that had been warmed in front of a fire. Then she felt Marcia's hand slide around her waist and onto her tummy. Now Marcia was stroking her again, but with her open hand.

And she was whispering. "April, you're lovely. I didn't . . . you're just lovely."

Then she felt Marcia's other hand reaching around, and both hands brush up her forearms near her face, and clutch both her wrists. Marcia gave a little tug. She didn't try to force her to lower her hands, but April knew what she wanted, and as much as she dreaded it, she allowed it to happen.

April's breasts were the freakiest part about her. They felt more like little flat pads than like pillows, but that wasn't the freaky part. It was her areolas. They were large, and light brown. And at odd times, they puffed up. They swelled up like bulging little breasts, but when you pushed them they'd go down, and then swell up again when you took your hand away.

Nobody knew about them. She didn't think even Mother knew. A lady doctor had looked at them, while giving her the team physical only six months ago, but hadn't said anything. That meant, April decided, that they were too strange to talk about. She never intended to tell anybody.

136

Now Marcia was feeling them. They were swollen, April could tell, although she didn't know why they got that way. Marcia pressed on one of them first, but when it went down she stopped pressing and started caressing it with her fingertips. Now both of them.

And now she was caressing one of her swollen areolas, and stroking her tummy with the other hand, and making little sounds.

It's not that it didn't feel good to April. She loved it, that Marcia was embracing her so apparently lovingly, after the cold treatment she'd given her earlier. And Marcia's height and gentle strength seemed to envelop April. If she'd been less nervous, she could tell, it would have given her a peaceful feeling.

It was just that she didn't really know what was going on. In order to prepare herself, while thinking about this possibility the night before, April had imagined several reactions Marcia might have, looking at her hairy tummy and puffy nipples for the first time. But this hadn't been one of them.

Finally, she pushed back with her elbows, to free herself, and turned around and took Marcia by the arms, to let her know she wasn't rejecting her. Marcia was looking kind of slack-jawed and lost, herself. She and April just stood there, close to each other, looking into each other's eyes. Neither of them said anything.

Then April became aware again of Marcia's breasts. It was hard not to—Marcia was several inches taller than April, which put her breasts almost at her neck, filling her vision, and with their upright nipples pointed at her face. Why not? April thought.

And she gently lifted one of them, from beneath. It was heavier than she'd expected. She started licking and feeling its nipple with her lips. She could feel it get even stiffer almost at once.

After a while, she felt Marcia's fingers under her chin, lifting her head. Marcia's face was very close to hers. Then Marcia put her hands on both sides of April's head and kissed her on the mouth.

It was April's first kiss, of that sort, from anyone. But it went all right. Marcia had caught her mouth just a little open, as it should be for a first kiss.

They held each other, then. This part felt very familiar and welcoming, after Marcia's strange and totally unexpected response to looking at her. April needed caring for, and apparently Marcia did too.

Suddenly, it occurred to April that they'd been at this for a while. She backed off and said, "Ned! I'll bet he's waiting for me!"

Marcia held her finger to her lips, and at the same time April heard somebody's feet shuffle outside their door, and stop in front of it. She reached down and grabbed her towel, and was wrapping it around her, when there was a tap on the door, and a lady's voice said, "Is everything okay in there?"

April went immediately to the door and opened it a little way, and squeezed out. "Yes, it's fine," she said, with a smile, to the lady standing there in her dripping bathing suit. "I was just helping my friend with a jammed zipper." She hoped Marcia's suit had a zipper. It had to, didn't it? Her own had a zipper.

"Oh, what a nuisance," said the lady. "Did you get it?"

138

"Yes," said April, at the same time that Marcia said, "Yes, we got it" from inside. These doors were incredibly thin, and had two- or three-inch spaces at the top and bottom.

April went into her own stall and dressed, and came out about the same time Marcia did. They linked arms, and squeezed each other close, and walked out together. "Quick thinking," said Marcia. In fact, April had tried to guess, while she was waiting in her own booth, what Marcia would do in such a situation, and had guessed that. She didn't think that *she* would be doing it.

Ned was waiting, and so was Marcia's ride, Dexter. The two boys were leaning against Ned's car and talking. April was caught up in a kind of wonder about what had just happened to her, but she also found herself intrigued about what these two guys would have to talk about, they seemed so different. But then she guessed that any two people could small-talk. And any two guys could talk about sports.

Ned made a point of looking at his watch. "You two can't get enough, can you?"

"Sorry," said Marcia cheerfully. "Running late." She went up to Dexter and gave him a hug, and they all waved good-bye.

On the way home, it occurred to April that she and Marcia were as different from each other as Ned and Dex were, and, as far as their lives were concerned, in almost the same way.

"Good swim?" asked Ned.

*   7   *

April stayed in her state of wonder for several days afterward, largely because she wanted to. Happiness was, after all, a big component of it. She had given up the notion of ever being actually *attractive* to anybody, and while she absorbed the warmth Marcia was surrounding her with, she scarcely believed it was real. She was afraid to look at Marcia's reaction too closely, for fear that she'd see it for what it really was—whatever that was. For now, she just wanted to enjoy her happiness.

But she knew she'd have to figure it out eventually. And she also knew that some day soon she'd have to answer some of the questions that kept popping into her head. Like, was what had happened between them sexual? She knew it probably was, although it had seemed to be something else—sort of just exploratory. And intimate, of course. The whole point was to get to know each other, intimately. To get close.

If it was sexual, she wondered, how did Dexter fit into Marcia's picture? And thinking of fitting in, what did this mean for April's life? Her direction for the past six months had been so clear and simple. She'd been alone, like Johnny Appleseed. This seemed to be a major departure—from everything April had known before now, even before her swimming started. It was certainly a major complication.

But the moment her mind would start to get very far into these matters, she would stop it. Not now, she thought.

April met Marcia every day for workout, and Marcia didn't seem to be in the least puzzled about their puzzling new relationship. She always seemed very happy to see April, and would always squeeze her arm close to her and, when there was no one around, would give her a little kiss on the cheek. And then she started whispering things like, "How's my furry little girlfriend?" April would giggle when she said those things, and would squeeze Marcia's arm in return. She could never think of anything clever enough about beautiful breasts to answer back.

But she loved her closeness with Marcia. And apparently she needed it. And she was almost sure Marcia did too. She's the one who had asked for it.

Without talking about it, the girls both apparently realized it would be too dangerous to keep looking at each other in the dressing stalls, and showering together. But by the weekend, April had started wanting to look at Marcia's breasts again. She just hadn't seen them enough, and she'd scarcely felt them at all. She thought Marcia wanted to see more of her too, but she wasn't sure.

And their kiss. April didn't feel any way about it while it was happening, except surprised. She spent the whole time while she was being kissed just getting used to the idea, and believing she was really being kissed. But later, she decided she liked it. At least she would like to try it again. Would Marcia want to kiss her again? She hoped she'd done it right.

That doubt was answered on the Saturday morning. Marcia actually telephoned her, just to talk. After some "What are you doing," and "Oh, just hanging around," Marcia said, "You know, we have a big problem."

"What's that?" said April, slightly alarmed. She got up and closed the kitchen door, quietly.

"We don't have anywhere to go."

"I know," April said. She knew exactly what Marcia meant. She'd been thinking about Lake Wagner, but it would be too risky. However secluded the area they found, somebody could blunder by at any time, and they'd be too nervous to enjoy being together. And anyway, how would they get there? And when? She told Marcia those things, and that she'd been hoping she could talk Ned into taking them again tomorrow, including Marcia. She really wanted to show it to her. She wasn't sure how they would manage all the bicycles. Would Marcia be able to come?

"Afternoon, I think so," Marcia said. "Morning's church. I have a standing date with Marilyn. My mother. And Dex, of course. Maybe Dex and I could meet you at the lake, in the afternoon. But you know, that doesn't solve our problem."

"No," said April.

"Next year we should be okay. We'll be driving. Are you taking drivers ed at school?"

April hadn't thought about it, but it seemed a good idea. "I don't guess there's any place at the Club?"

"No, no!" Marcia seemed horrified. "Can you imagine what would happen to us if we got caught?"

April couldn't imagine, until she thought about what might happen to Mother's application for membership. But she knew she didn't like the whole idea of "getting caught." Not just that she didn't want to get caught—of course she didn't—but that other people thought it was their business. As if they were kids smoking in the bathroom.

"There's only one good place, but it's not so good," said Marcia. "At home."

The idea seemed perfect to April. The home that came into her mind was Marcia's. It was what April would call a mansion, with lots of rooms, and big grounds. There must be some corner, somewhere . . .

"Of course, my house won't work," continued Marcia. "Rolanda's there all day, and she's always poking around everywhere. And old Gilbert. And Marilyn is in and out. And your place is even worse, with your mother and Ned and now Helen coming and going at all hours."

"But . . . Marcia, I don't know what you're saying. Are you saying there's no way? And that we may as well give up the idea?" April had seen a possible solution. But she had to be sure Marcia really wanted it.

"Oh, no, of course I'm not saying that. I know we'll finally get together again some way. I just don't know how."

"Well," said April, "Maybe you're right. You don't have a way to get here, do you?"

"There? Well, of course I do. It depends when."

"Any morning," said April. "Any weekday morning."

"What do you mean?"

"Ned starts football this Monday morning. And every morning is Mother's office time, at her office, when she's not showing. She does all her business stuff mornings. And we don't have any Rolandas or Gilberts. But how would you . . ."

"April! That's brilliant! My bicycle! Marilyn hasn't said I *can't!* Of course, I'll come see you! Oh, April, that's wonderful!"

"Isn't it . . . dangerous?"

"What? Oh, the bicycle? No, course not. Dex and I used to ride the roads all the time, til we got tired of it. Sidewalks, mainly. Look, what time should I get there Monday?"

And so it was decided. No workout this Monday. That was a problem, since Mother was supposed to take her to the Club on the way to work, and she would read until she could pick her up lunchtime. She'd have to figure out what to tell Mother, but she'd come up with an excuse. Marcia would pedal over, and leave by noon. They would set up something they were doing together in case somebody showed up unexpectedly. Marcia said she'd bring some photos of the swimming team in her backpack, and they would start a scrapbook.

It was quite a long ride from Marcia's house. She must really want to come. And April wanted her to. She just couldn't believe it would really work out.

April was certain things like this were supposed to sort of *happen*. People didn't plan them. If you planned them, and you knew what you were going to do, then it wasn't just an accident, was it? Not that April really knew. But every time she thought of the idea that somebody might be out to "catch them," she became more determined to go through with it, whatever it was.

What she did know was that she was so excited throughout the whole weekend that she couldn't dwell on their plans. She couldn't keep from thinking about them, either, but it was as if too much thinking about them would jinx them somehow. Now she wished they hadn't decided to postpone their lake outing, just because they'd figured out another way to get together. It would have passed some of the time, and seeing Marcia would have taken the edge off. Instead, she spent another weekend trying to concentrate on her book, while her mind irresistibly wandered, requiring her to order it back into line like a stern grade-school teacher with a wild kid. She'd never guessed that reading would require more discipline than a workout.

She made her mother happy by saying that she and Marcia had decided to take some time off from swimming these last few weeks of the summer. Nothing regular. When they felt they needed a rest-day, they'd just take one. Like tomorrow. They needed an even longer break than the weekend gave them. Dexter and Marcia might come over, and they'd go out for some coffee.

When Marcia did show up the next morning on her bicycle, April almost couldn't take it. Shyness overcame her. If she could have gone back in time to cancel the whole thing, she thought she would have. She saw Marcia ride up, and head straight up the drive to the back, as planned. She ran downstairs to open the garage door. But when she closed the door, she couldn't bear to stand there alone with Marcia, in the garage, so she sort of ran away, calling over her shoulder, "C'mon up."

Marcia followed her up the stairs to her room. She dumped the contents of her backpack on the bed. "Okay," she said. "Here's my idea for a scrapbook." She started laying out photos and clippings on the desk. April cleared her some more space.

"Oh, I have some of those," said April. "See?" She gestured at her corkboard, where she had pinned some of the same photos and clippings, mostly of the school polo team. A photo of Marcia was displayed prominently.

"Oh, I have a better one for you than that," said Marcia.

As far as April could tell, there was no way in the world they were going to phase from scrapbook to something less objective.

But Marcia took care of it. She took April by the arm, and turned her so they were facing. April thought she was going to get kissed. She would have welcomed it, just as a relief from the staggering intensity. But instead, Marcia said, "Darling, I'm all sweaty from the ride. Let's take a quick shower! Just a rinse-off, okay?"

April was in no frame of mind to resist any clear order from Marcia. She nodded, and watched as Marcia started taking off her clothes. After half a minute, she got the idea, and started taking her own off too. There were Marcia's lovely big breasts, flopping out of her size "C" bra. Then Marcia got down on one knee, and pulled down April's jeans, and then her panties. She leaned forward and kissed April's tummy, but then she immediately stood up. April stepped out of her jeans and panties, and they were both naked. April could see they'd taken a major step in phasing away from the scrapbook.

They turned and April led the way into the bathroom. She adjusted the shower, and then got out a couple of towels and threw a couple of washrags in. Then she got in herself, and held her hand out to Marcia. She was catching on.

Marcia smiled and stepped into the spray, and immediately gave April a hug. Then she grabbed one of the rags and put some liquid soap on it, and turned April around and washed her back and butt. She handed April the rag, and then she turned around, and April did the same for her. She marveled at how firm and muscular Marcia's butt was, and reasoned that her own must be the same. Then Marcia took the rag back, renewed the soap, and slowly washed April's front, starting with her chest, with their puffed-up nipples, and on down to her tummy, and then between her legs, where she lathered abundantly. She handed the rag to April, who followed suit. April couldn't help but imagine, while she was washing Marcia's breasts, what it would be like to wash her own chest with those on it. At least her own nipples were all puffed up now, so there was something there.

April was getting the impression Marcia knew what she was doing, and that relaxed her a little bit. All she would really have to do is follow suit.

As if prompted, Marcia stepped out of the shower, leaving April to turn it off. Then she handed April out. She had already grabbed a towel, and she patted and rubbed April gently all over, and April got the other towel and did the same to Marcia. April walked over to the open door and listened. She was sure she would hear somebody come in now, but with the shower on . . . All was quiet.

"So what are the chances?" Marcia asked. "Of your mother . . ."

"She never has," said April. "Even when she isn't feeling well, she stays at work."

Marcia walked up beside her and put her hand on her back, and stepped close, making sure her nipples rubbed against her shoulder. April was recognizing that she did that deliberately. With her other hand she started stroking her tummy, with its damp hair. The first time she'd done that, at the Club, April had no idea what to think or feel. But in the past week it had sunk in that Marcia found her tummy attractive.

148

And now that she knew that, the attention excited her. She started touching Marcia's most accessible breast, gently squeezing and massaging it as she had imagined doing all the week before, feeling its weight and glancing at it afresh every few seconds to let its size impress her. She had experimented with her own nipples several times last week to find out what felt good, so she knew to touch the nipple every few moves. And, again as if on cue, it stiffened.

Marcia was doing something else April must have noticed the time before, because she thought about that, too, during the week. She was radiating. When she started feeling April's tummy hair, and again when April started feeling her breast, she felt a wave of heat flash from Marcia's body. Since April was naked too, she could feel it easily. It was unmistakable. April wondered if Marcia knew that she did that. And she wondered if she radiated too.

The first time she had felt it, she realized, was when they were just walking along together after one of their swims, and April did a sudden turn to point at a cardinal that flew past, by accident striking Marcia quite hard in the chest, just above her breasts, with her outstretched hand. April was overcome with remorse, and gushed apologies, but Marcia wasn't hurt. But later April remembered the sudden heat wave that followed the blow, and wondered about it.

April became aware, now, that Marcia was doing something different. Her tummy strokes were getting lower, down into April's big heap of pubic hair. She was touching the top of her vagina, whether intentionally April didn't know; but she did know it was making her weak-kneed. She started wobbling toward the bed, murmuring "I want . . . to . . ."

But Marcia sat on the bed herself, and held April in front of her. She leaned over and started nuzzling and kissing April around her navel, every now and then sticking her tongue into it. Then she was on her knees, on the floor, burying her face in April's pubic hair, and . . .

Licking! April could feel her tongue on her skin, feeling around . . . at the top of her vagina . . . lower . . .

April couldn't stand. She leaned over with a moan, and collapsed on her hands on the bed, then crawled almost over Marcia in among the stuffed toys, and rolled onto her back. Marcia was lying beside her immediately, half on top of her, looking with concern into her face. "Darling, are you all right?" she said.

"Yes . . . yes," said April. "Now I'm lying down, I'm okay." She laughed a weak little laugh. And she put her arms around Marcia and pulled her to her and kissed her. She hadn't had her kiss yet! They kissed a long time, again and again. They were feeling each other's breasts, and groaning little groans.

"Oh, Darling, I've missed you so much this week!" said Marcia, leaning on one elbow, while continuing to stroke April's puffy breast with her thumb. Then she did a little laugh of her own. "Even when I was with you sometimes I was missing you!"

That bothered April a little. "I missed you too," she said.

"But not when I was with you!"

Marcia laughed again. "Oh, I know. I need . . . I don't know. I'm never close enough. I mean . . . I'm very needy. I get . . . worried. I need too much reassurance. And April, I know . . . I know you care for me, too. You're just more dedicated to your workouts. Oh, I'm dedicated too, but . . . you know. I was surprised you were willing to skip it today."

April understood what Marcia needed her to say. "I needed you too," she said. And then she added, with another little chuckle, "Darling!" And she pulled Marcia down and kissed her again. Then they just gazed at each other for a while.

This gazing, right now, is the way April had imagined it would be. They were going to look at each other. And feel close. Touch. Not that she minded the licking. Marcia wanted to do it, and she knew, when she got over the surprise, it would be like the stroking and kissing. She would want it, too. And until she understood more about this, she'd decided to do what Marcia wanted.

Marcia was still gazing into her eyes, now, but her hand was back on her tummy. It felt good, again. Now April knew how a puppy or an old tabby cat felt. She knew why it purred.

But then Marcia kissed her again, with a kind of urgency she hadn't recognized before. She was kissing her mouth quite hard. And then she slid her hand over her pubic hair, down between her legs, and gave a little squeeze. She did it again, this time crossing her leg over April's, and pushing her hand under her back and around her shoulders, and pulling her tighter against her. It was as though she was holding her in place.

April knew she wasn't really. She knew she could get up if she wanted to. And if she didn't feel so weak. She just felt that she was in a strong grip—a feeling she had had before with Marcia. But this time, the grip conveyed a sort of desperation, a need and a determination to satisfy it, that April hadn't experienced from Marcia before.

So she just lay there, on her back, her eyes closed, while Marcia squeezed her vagina again and again. It occurred to her that there was no doubt, now, that what they were doing was sexual. It didn't make any difference. April couldn't do anything about it. She couldn't move. She was trapped in some kind of spell, and didn't want out.

After a while she felt Marcia's finger slip inside her a little way. She could tell she was very wet, as she sometimes used to get just thinking about Robbie or some other boy. Now Marcia was stroking her mainly with her finger. She worked it toward the top of her vagina, through the tangles, and started touching around on what April knew was her clit, although she'd never stroked it like that. Now she started feeling the urgency within herself that Marcia had obviously been feeling.

"Oooo," said Marcia. "It's big."

What's big? April wanted to ask, but couldn't respond with anything but a sort of slurred mutter. Maybe should be doing something to Marcia too. Don't know what to do. Squeezing

152

her leg with hand now, sometimes, when I think of it. Can't move now. Later maybe. But now I am moving, doing dolphin kick. Whole bed moving, like a wave. Marcia insisting, insisting. So lovely, such beautiful breasts, I should be doing something to her, but she's doing it all to me . . . Oh. Oh.

April felt a little vibration inside her, focused between her legs. It seemed natural, and good, although she'd never felt it before. She lay still. The bed was still. After a minute, she realized she'd relaxed. She'd felt a kind of relief the moment it happened. She thought she could move again.

Then she realized something else. Marcia had stopped rubbing her.

She looked up at Marcia, and was surprised at her expression. Open-eyed, and nearly open mouthed.

"What's wrong?" asked April, alarmed.

"What . . . what did you do?" Marcia said.

"What did I do?" asked April, even more alarmed.

Marcia shook her head, even more open-eyed. "I can't . . . I can't . . ." she said, and then lapsed into silence, but then grabbed April in a big hug, and held on. April hugged her back. She had no idea what she'd done, or even what Marcia was talking about. But she was very anxious to right any wrong, if she could.

She let Marcia hug her, and sort of squirm against her, for a long time, and she squirmed back. Any hug from Marcia, she'd come to understand, prominently featured the big pillow of her breasts, and was worth dwelling on. Then they kissed some more. Obviously Marcia wasn't in any hurry to tell her what she'd done wrong.

Finally April said, "Marcia, Darling?"

"Yes, April Darling?" responded Marcia.

"I want to feel you. Between your legs. Like you did me. Please."

"I'd love for you to do that, Darling," said Marcia. "But April, I'm . . . I'm not like you."

April had to ponder that for a moment. Finally she said, "I know you're not like me, Darling. That's why I'd love to feel you."

Marcia laughed and rolled over on her back. For the first time April saw her breasts in that position, and was newly impressed. They sagged slightly out on the sides, but primarily they were big slightly flattened hills, sitting invitingly on Marcia's chest, with their nipples like bullseyes a little above the centers. April quite definitely had nothing like them on her own chest. She had unknowingly trained herself, over the past half-year or longer, to ignore other people's attractive features. Now the realization that those lovely mounds were *hers,* in a way, naked and available for her to look at and touch and feel and lick if she wanted to, overwhelmed her anew.

So she did that. She licked and squeezed the nipples between her lips, and felt them stiffen again. Then she reached down and began stroking Marcia's little patch of hair, and then further down, squeezing her vagina, following Marcia's own agenda. Marcia laughed again for some reason, then, after a

154

while, she started moaning and doing a little dolphin kick of her own, even though butterfly wasn't her stroke. April kept licking and sucking Marcia's nipples at the same time she was squeezing her.

Then April's middle finger slipped inside automatically, making Marcia jerk a little and shove her hips forward, interrupting her dolphin kick. April moved her finger toward the top of Marcia's vagina, as Marcia had done to her, searching for her clit. At first she couldn't find it; but then she located the place it should be, and felt something there. So that's what was big, in her own vagina. She started rubbing her finger around, and, little clit or not, there was no doubt that Marcia could feel it. Now Marcia's dolphin kick was back, and she was making rhythmic moaning noises.

It was making April very excited, too, all over again. She found she was enjoying Marcia's reaction almost as much as she had enjoyed her own. Just the fact that she could give her so much pleasure pleased her.

After a while, Marcia's moans started coming faster and faster, and finally her hips pumped in three or four big, slow lunges, as she made a long continuous moan. Then she lay still. April didn't recognize that as anything she'd done herself, but she guessed she was supposed to stop rubbing, even though she hadn't felt Marcia's little shudder. Maybe you can't feel it with your hand, April thought. Maybe Marcia hadn't felt April's either.

Marcia grabbed her in a huge hug, and rolled over on top of her, kissing her all over her face, and muttering, "Oh, Darling," again and again, and making April smile. Finally April smacked

155

her on her bottom to get her to stop, making Marcia laugh and roll over again on her back.

The two girls lay there side by side panting lightly. April felt very easy and assured of Marcia's friendship, and she thought, as she lay there beside her, how much better it was to have a friend than to make herself do without. She just hadn't known it was possible for her.

"Darling," said Marcia, "I have a favor to ask."

"Anything," said April.

"You'll do it?"

"Don't know til you ask," said April.

"You said anything," said Marcia.

"You can *ask* anything."

"Stop shaving your arms," said Marcia.

"My arms? Why?" April was surprised, although she'd have thought she'd be over surprises by now.

"You'll be even sexier. And you won't scratch me up so much. I bet I'm all bloody."

Hmm. Sexier? Stranger and stranger. But not worse and worse. Just impossible, probably. What would Mother say? What about their contract? "What about my legs?" said April, buying time to think about it. "Don't they scratch you too?"

"Maybe so," said Marsha, "but *my* legs can scratch back." She giggled. "April?"

"Yes?"

"Is it your mother?

April paused. "Yeah," she finally said. "She won't like me with furry arms. I'm not sure *I* will." Then *she* giggled.

"Then wait a month. When you're wearing long sleeves. And always wear a robe or something around here. That should give you the winter to figure out what to tell her."

"And a month to figure out what to tell you," said April.

Then they both giggled.

Before Marcia left, they had plotted what they would tell people who asked about time they spent together. April wondered what to tell her mother, who was sure to ask how she'd spent the morning. "Tell her I came over," said Marcia. "We had some coffee. And talked. In fact, we did talk, didn't we? Let's have some coffee now. I can use some anyway. If my mother asks, I'll tell her the same thing." April asked her if Dexter had come with her. "Dexter? No. You know he didn't. He was golfing. That's what he does nearly every morning." Then how had she got here? "On my bicycle. You know that too. I got here when I got here, and left when I left. But only if it comes up."

April began to understand the only way she'd normally have to change her stories was by leaving things out. That made her feel a little better about putting more distance between herself and her mother, although she knew that the existing distance was already unbridgeable.

Marcia said a puzzling thing before she pedaled away. She kissed April goodbye, and said, "I'm glad you chose me." April couldn't figure out what she meant, before she was gone. She remembered, if anything, that Marcia had chosen *her.*

After April had waved goodbye, and closed the garage door, she went up and took her third shower of the morning. She needed one, she thought, and anyway, it would enable her to explain the extra towel. She'd got sweaty taking a fast walk with Marcia. But only if it came up.

This was a new way of thinking for April. She'd never so obviously and systematically lied to her mother before, although her whole manner had, in a way, been a lie for a while. And now Ned was also on the other side of that wall she was building. That bothered her even more. The only person she could trust with her whole life was Marcia.

And yet, Marcia had a whole life that April wasn't a part of. Her whole Dexter-Club-Club friends-parents life. Thinking about that, April realized that Marcia was already quite skilled in maintaining these separate lives. She knew just how many lies she had to tell, just where she had to make the dam watertight, and where she could let a few leaks through.

But these thoughts didn't bother April much, because her feeling of wonder still presided over her life—a life that had completely transformed in a week. It was almost as if she herself had been transfigured—the very features of her body that she'd been convinced, only a week earlier, made her a pariah, an untouchable, were now the basis of her confidence in her hold on Marcia. At least as surprising was her realization that she wanted and needed a hold on Marcia.

She had to figure out what it all meant, but whatever she figured, she felt like the ugly duckling after it realized it was a swan. And she knew that nothing else, for years, had made her quite so happy.

*   8   *

April's summer of love was rapidly coasting to its finish. She and Marcia had a few more swimming workouts, and what talk they could get in before and after. They decided they'd better not repeat Marcia's visit to April's house too frequently. It would be too obvious a change from their known routines. Some neighbor might casually comment to Mother. They'd do it once a week, on different days, and figure out a new routine when school started.

April was getting excited about school—the polo team as well as new classes. The fact that she would have a close friend beside her going into the new school gave her a warm feeling of confidence. She tried to talk about her anticipation with Marcia, but couldn't seem to get her to share in her excitement. Marcia continued to say loving things, and April responded in kind. But April found herself needing more time with Marcia, without the workout routine preoccupying their attention. Not just for lovemaking, but also for conversation and just being together.

April finally managed to arrange their ride around Lake Wagner that she'd been longing for. It was a week before the start of school, and they skipped their morning swim in favor of afternoon cycling. Ned and Helen were supposed to go, but they decided the Autumn breeze was too "nippy" for them. But otherwise it was a crystal blue day, and April knew the trees would be trying on their bright colors, so she talked Ned into taking her and Marcia and coming back to get them—although he said he might have to leave them there longer than an hour. They agreed to wait for him where he dropped them off, after their ride.

Neither of them wanted much to ride too fast, and certainly not to race or otherwise compete. They pedaled just fast enough to stay warm. April was completely at peace. The changing colors and crisp views and sparkles on the water combined with the easy exercise, and with just being with Marcia, to give April a feeling of perfect fulfillment. And Marcia, April felt, had to be sharing that feeling with her. She said it was a beautiful and relaxing place, as April had promised.

Only toward the end of their ride did it occur to April that Marcia seemed distracted. She'd said little, and her laughs seemed subdued. Occasionally April thought she saw a disturbed expression on her face. April decided not to question it—just to wait until Marcia was ready.

But she did have a question, which she decided to ask, to pass the time while they were sitting at the picnic table waiting for Ned. "You know, when we were making love," she said. "You

160

asked me what I'd done. I don't guess I understood. What were you talking about?"

Marcia looked puzzled. "What you'd done?"

"Yeah, it kind of bothered me. I couldn't think of anything I'd done. It was right after you . . .you rubbed me."

"Oh, yeah," Marcia said, with a little laugh April was glad to hear. "Your climax. Your orgasm. It's like a boy's."

"A boy's?" April couldn't hide the slight alarm in her voice.

"Oh, it's good, don't worry. Only about half of women can do it. All of them wish they could. I read about it once in one of Dexter's magazines. I'm pretty sure that's what they were talking about."

"So . . ." said April. "Can you do it?"

Marcia made a wistful expression. "I don't know. I never have. Maybe. They say it comes later with some of us."

"But I know you did *something*. You had some sort of climax. I'm sure of it. Didn't it feel good?"

"Oh, yes, Darling. You made me feel very good. But it's . . . different. I sort of get high. And everything else sort of . . . goes away. The rest of the world. Except you didn't go away. It all had to do with you. And I get . . . you know, higher and higher. And then I'm, sort of, over it. The world comes back."

April thought about it. Marcia's description seemed very close to her own experience, except she remembered, maybe, thinking about it more while it was happening. Figuring it out. But still, it seemed the same. "Yes," she said. "That's what happened to me. It wasn't different."

"But you do something else. A little vibration. Don't you remember?"

"Well . . . yes, maybe. Don't you do that? I didn't *do* it. Not deliberately. It just happened. It doesn't feel like a big difference."

"The same as boys. They have an actual . . . uh . . . muscular . . . sort of, incident. Event. When they ejaculate. Every time! It's not fair! Then they're finished. And you do it too! Course, you don't ejaculate. I guess you don't. But . . ."

April wanted to ask some more questions, although she knew she'd have to do some reading too, before she understood it. But it occurred to her that this was a perfect opportunity to ask something else she'd been wondering about. She knew she was taking a chance. It was none of her business. Marcia had made that pretty clear by never talking about it. But she thought it had something to do with her own place in Marcia's life. And she felt encouraged by their closeness—that any mistake could be repaired. So she blundered on into it.

"So, uh . . . so, how do you know? That boys do it every time? Does Dexter do it? I mean, do you do it to him?"

"Oh, yes, of course. I have to."

"*Have* to?"

"They expect it. Older boys expect it. I have to do it with my hand. And sometimes with my mouth. If you want to keep your boyfriend, you have to do it."

"But, you make it sound like . . . I mean, don't you enjoy it?"

"Not much. At first, I guess it was exciting. The newness. But it's only enjoyable when it's loving. When it has to do with love. For a while, I thought that was what it was about. But boys don't understand love. I mean, they love sex, of course. They have to have that orgasm. And if you want to keep them, that's what you have to give them. But it's just a chore. He doesn't even play with my breasts much any more. My 'tits.' And he never rubs me, like you did. We did."

"But . . . don't you love Dexter?"

"Ha!" said Marcia. "I guess I like him, most of the time. Except when he gets too demanding. I just need him. Or I will, some day. Or some other man, like him. But it's not love. Boys don't understand love."

April was the one who didn't understand. Didn't Ned understand love? She was sure Ned loved her. But this other thing Marcia was talking about was . . . something else. April felt way out of her depth.

And that's the reason, and for no other reason, April asked the next question.

"Do you think we love each other?" she asked. "You and I?"

There was a pause, and a stare. And then: "Yes we love each other!" So loud April first thought Marcia was angry. And she

163

may have been, partly. But as April looked at her, she saw that another emotion had caused the explosion. Tears were filling Marcia's eyes, and rolling down her cheeks. "How can you say that?" she said, still very loudly, her voice breaking. "After our time together. Of course we love each other!"

"Oh, I know, I know!" said April, and jumped up and stepped around the table and put her arm around Marcia as she sat beside her. "I know that, Darling," she said again. "I was just trying to understand . . . Marcia, Darling, at least I know I love you. I really do. Very much."

That was intended to stop the crying, but it had the opposite effect. Marcia started bawling. April didn't know what to do. She just sat with her arm around her. She found a handkerchief in her pocket and used it to dab the tears as they continued to flow, abundantly. April said a few dumb things, like "Marcia, what is it?" and "Don't cry, Darling." But it did no good. Marcia cried and cried. April had never known anyone to cry like that. Certainly no one in her family did it.

She had stopped bawling, but was still sniffling, when Ned drove up and walked over. "What happened?" he asked. "Did you hurt yourself?"

"No, no," April responded. "We're okay." Marcia didn't answer.

April led Marcia to the back seat, and then helped Ned mount the bikes on Helen's parents' rack, which had found a new home on top of Ned's car. She shrugged in response to Ned's enquiring expression. Then she got in back with Marcia, and put her arm around her again. Once again, Marcia started crying, but managed to stop after a few miles. They drove back to Marcia's house in near-silence, and Ned unloaded her blue bicycle for her.

"I'm so sorry," said Marcia to Ned, shaking his hand. "I was upset. Thanks so much."

"Sure," said Ned. "Hope you feel better."

"Bye, April," said Marcia. "Thank you too. I enjoyed it very much."

April gave her a little hug, but not a long one, for fear it would make her cry some more. That seemed to be the way things were working. "I'll call you later," she said. "See you tomorrow."

"What was that all about?" asked Ned, when they were on their way.

"Oh, boyfriend trouble," said April.

"Oh. I'm not surprised," said Ned. "That Dex character seems to be a snobbish bastard. Course, I don't really know him."

In fact, April had no idea what was going on with Marcia. She didn't know yet that that evening, and the next day, would complete her introduction to a new way of looking at the world, and its forces and uncertainties, and possibly its dangers. Maybe even its protections and repairs. Whatever she got from it, it would round out her summer education.

Fortunately, April didn't have to wait long to learn almost the whole story. She later realized what a boon that was, although it gave her far too much to think about all at once. It would take her several days just to get it straight. But if she'd been left in the dark about any bits of the story, it might have driven her crazy. Well, maybe that's an exaggeration. April was pretty tough. But at least it could have left her very bitter. And of course, allowing that to happen is always a mistake.

Her mother was the primary messenger. "Hi Honey," she greeted April. "Enjoy the ride?"

"We did, yes," said April, "except . . ." She hesitated. She didn't know whether it was right to tell Mother or not. But she decided it couldn't do any harm, since she didn't really have much to tell. And since Ned would probably mention it anyway. "Except, Marcia was a little upset about something."

"Really? Upset? I'd have thought she'd have been excited. Although . . . Marilyn did say she might be a little . . . uh . . . 'unsettled,' I think she said. Anyway, what do you think about Palmerston?"

The word didn't register right away with April. She'd heard it before. Finally it clicked. It was a fancy prep school in a little town with the same name, a couple hours north. Catholic. The subject of a lot of class jokes among girls she knew. A boarding school. "Palmerston—the school? A girls' school, right?" Mother was nodding. "Okay, what about it?"

"Uh-oh," Mother said. "She didn't tell you."

A fear seized April like a huge icy hand around her chest. "Tell me what?" she managed to choke out.

"Marcia's going there."

Going there. Marcia. "When?"

"I don't know exactly when. This week sometime. Term starts next week, I think. Same as public high school."

"You mean . . . she's going to *school* there? She's not going to our high school?"

"Well, yes, of course, that's what I mean. She's going to Palmerston, not to our city high school."

April sank down. Fortunately there was a kitchen chair to catch her.

"You didn't know, did you," said Mother.

"I . . . no," said April. She still didn't believe it. Mother didn't really know either. Although the way Marcia had acted suggested something was seriously wrong. But if it were so settled, why *didn't* April know? Why *hadn't* Marcia told her?

"Well, Marilyn said she didn't want to go," Mother continued. "In fact, she said she flat *refused* to go. Until Sunday— let's see, yesterday—when she—Marilyn—and George sat her down and showed her that she really had no choice . . ."

"No choice? How could she have no choice?"

"Oh, Honey. That's a question only a child who's been given lots of freedom could ask. Lots of protected freedom. Maybe too much. I suppose I should be proud of that, about you. I *am* proud of you. You're becoming—have become—your own person. But when you're underage, in the care of your parents or guardians, they have lots of ways of making you do what they think is best for you. Even more ways when they're as rich and influential as the Martindales."

"But *why* would they force her to do something she didn't want to do?" April was in what is known as the "denial stage."

"Well, Marilyn was very open and honest with me. She feels Marcia had come too much under your influence."

"*My* influence? My *influence?*"

"Marilyn says that Marcia has always been very easily influenced by strong-willed friends. Like yourself. She pointed out that Marcia has neglected all her other friends—everyone except Dexter—to swim with you. I had to agree that was probably so. You *have* become very single-minded about that, you know. Not that she blames *you*—Marilyn and George don't blame you. They admire your single-mindedness. And as I said, I can't help but admire it myself, although I also can't help but worry that you're neglecting other equally important things. Like your social skills. Although I don't have any serious complaints about that, yet. But your sort of dedication isn't suitable for everyone, and I understand, very well, why the Martindales might decide to step in . . ."

"Palmerston. Now. No, I don't believe it. Why didn't she tell me?" But even as she spoke, she knew why. She couldn't. She probably intended to, but the betrayal was too overwhelming. Marcia was a coward.

April felt anger against Marcia rising within her. Was Marcia blaming her for what happened between them?

"Anyway," Mother continued, "several of Marcia's long-time friends will be going there, so she won't be alone. People from the Club. You probably know who they are. All good families, of course. And, April—Marilyn Martindale wants to talk to you. Don't worry—she just wants to explain things. She knows you'll be upset. I told her you'll understand. I said I'd get you to give her a call whenever you're ready. So, do you think you're ready to hear what she has to say?"

April managed to stand up. "No," she said. "I'm not ready." She turned and walked toward the hall stairs. "I may never be ready."

"Please, April . . ." said Mother, but she stopped there, and April continued up to her room. She closed the door and flopped onto her bed. The memories that arose like a cloud of dust from the covers and the stuffed toys weren't from her childhood. They were from another occasion, a few weeks before. Bitter memories. She wondered if Marcia knew then.

Suddenly, a new understanding of Marcia swept over her. Gone was the loving Marcia—loving because she needed love so desperately, and extravagantly capable of giving it in return. In her place was a self-centered, manipulative person, whose privileged upbringing had taught her to take whatever she wanted, without regret, from anyone she considered beneath her. She knew all along she wasn't going to the vulgar worker's school up the road. She was going to the posh school, with all her *real* friends. People in her social class. "Good families." Meaning "rich and influential."

And the last couple of months? Marcia just needed to fill in a boring summer, and so she offered a naive local girl a glittering temporary place at her "Club" in return for a little weirdo sex and some free physical training. Something odd and different. She would probably have a good laugh, at her new school with her *real* lover, a normal pretty girl like Marcia herself, about the freakish furry creature she'd seduced, for fun, back in town. Suddenly April felt a surge of remorse at her own stupidity, showing her body to Marcia in that way. And then—when Marcia's mother guessed what she'd been up to, Marcia had blamed April!

April let her reconstruction of her friend's image run its course, and stewed for a little while. But she felt very uneasy about it. She'd seen other girls do that when they'd broken up with their boyfriends. They'd put their memories of their exes through malicious makeovers, turning the people they'd loved, not long before, into monsters, and filling their own lives with hate. April had always thought that was dumb—yet here she was, doing it herself! Even in her frantic state, April could think of evidence that her new picture of Marcia as demon was wrong. Could Marcia have cried so persuasively, if she hadn't meant it? Why was she upset at all? And why did Mother say that Marilyn didn't blame her? Blame April?

Blame her for what?

But . . . if that new image of Marcia *wasn't* Marcia, what was? Who was she really? And why hadn't she told her she was leaving, when she clearly did know, this afternoon? Could she maybe have seen what it would be like, if she'd told her? *Two hysterical teenagers,* all alone by the lake, with no referee or psychologist in sight!

The only way she could find out what was really going on, she decided after an hour's mental, as well as bodily, tossing and turning, was to talk to Marcia. She jumped up from the bed, and was almost to the door of her room, before she stopped. Mother would hear any telephone conversation. She couldn't talk freely. Marcia lived too far away for her to get there before it was too late, and anyway Marilyn would answer the door. Or her father! She imagined herself throwing gravel at Marcia's bedroom window, which was ridiculous enough to make her flop back down on her bed.

And there she lay, for hours—she had no idea how many—imagining and dismissing the various conspiracies various villains had concocted against her, and sometimes against her and Marcia, sometimes barely resisting a wild hatred for the conspirators. Mother plotting with Marilyn. Marilyn plotting with Marcia. Maybe they needed some excuse to prevent Mother from joining the Club! April hadn't thought about that! In that case, they really were a hateful bunch.

And there was always the dark possibility that Marilyn and George had guessed what was going on between their daughter and April. She was sure Mother didn't suspect.

She heard a gentle tap at her door, and decided to pretend she was asleep. She heard the door open, then close again, quietly.

Finally the misery she'd been warding off found its way past her safeguards, and she settled, without resistance, into sorrow for herself. She cried some then, quietly, although she couldn't entirely stifle a few sobs. She dozed briefly, and awoke to a painful awareness of the extent of her loss. Her *only* close companion. Her swimming buddy, and teammate! Her . . . lover. She knew that nobody else in the world would ever be attracted to her, or do the things to her she'd so quickly come to need, or respond with such intensity to the things she'd learned to do in return. She would be far better off if she'd never experienced those things. She lay still a while, stunned by her grief, before sleeping restlessly.

At some point she had the half-waking idea that, after all, she might see Marcia again, maybe often. They wouldn't be that far away from each other. She seized on that hope, and was able to get a few hours sleep before dawn.

*   9   *

April's next day, after the devastating news, was spent trying to get away from thinking about it. She decided to go in for her usual morning workout, even though the Club now felt like an alien world to her, on the theory that if the whole thing were some sort of hoax Marcia would be there too. Or maybe Marcia wanted to talk to her, or at least knew she wanted to talk to Marcia, and so would show up out of kindness. But Marcia didn't show up, and April ended up taking a fast, hard swim after her warmup, changing strokes for each length. She was out of the pool in half the usual time, and spent the other half sitting on the bench outside, waiting for Ned, and trying and pretending to read.

Ned already knew what had happened, and he acted casual about it. Maybe he *was* casual about it. Boys don't understand love.

Mother was home earlier than usual, and tried to keep April occupied with conversation. April was grateful, and managed to get into some of her old household routines with her. There were some setbacks. Like, when Mother asked, "April, did you two—you and Marcia—did you get up to any mischief together? At the club? Like, did you smoke, or anything like that?"

"No, Mother, of course not!" April responded, relaxing from her sudden wariness. "We were trying to be athletes! Why? Did anybody say we did?"

"No, no, Honey. Not at all. I'm just trying to get the whole picture myself. I actually think that the Martindales' decision had less to do with you than I suggested yesterday. I'm sure there were many good reasons for sending Marcia to Palmerston. It's a good school, after all."

By late afternoon, April was ready to talk to Marilyn Martindale, if only to pick up what information she could from the conversation. Plain confirmation of Mother's story would dismiss half her uncertainty.

Mother was delighted. "I'll call her now," she said. "She should be home." Before April could panic and change her mind, Mother had made the connection and handed her the phone.

"Hel . . . hello? This is April," she got out.

"Hello, Sweety. I'm very pleased to hear from you. I asked your mother to tell you I was very anxious to talk to you, to explain our decision about Marcia and Palmerston. I know you two had become closest friends, and if you were half as upset about it as she was, you could probably use some explanation."

"Yes. Thank you. It came as a shock," said April, sitting in the nearby kitchen chair.

"Well, I wish the shock part could have been avoided. But you know, Marcia resisted our decision for weeks, until finally Mr. Martindale had to just put his foot down, at the last minute."

"I see," said April. What Marilyn was saying was, for some twisted reason, making her feel better.

"I want to make it perfectly clear that we don't disapprove of you, in any way. In fact, you've picked up a sizeable following at the Club—you have some real fans there—and I want you to know I'm one of them. I'm not trying to polish you up, or whatever that saying is. It's just that Alice—your mother told me earlier today what she told you, and I'm trying to reassure you that we consider your friendship with Marcia a real benefit for her, and we're grateful for it. There's no doubt she can benefit from being close to someone as . . .as disciplined and . . . dedicated as you are. I mean

. . . I mean, the last thing I would want to do is keep you two apart permanently, although I do think Marcia needs to focus, now, on getting ready for school. Mentally as well as in the ordinary ways. Do you see?"

"Yes ma'am. I think so," said April. Just as she should.

"You know, I heard a comment about you recently, that I'd like to pass on. I don't know if you knew this, but Mr. Henderson, your teacher . . . your history teacher last year, is the son of a couple of our members, and oldest friends—Arnold and Clarisse Henderson. Anyway, he was at our table at the Club, with his parents, you know, and we were discussing Marcia's . . . resistance to our plan to send her to Palmerston, and your name came up, and he immediately interjected, "Ah, yes, one of my best students!" I don't believe I told your mother that story, but I'll be sure to do so. Although I'd never thought of you in that way, I wasn't in the least surprised.

"Anyway, as you may know, Marcia hasn't performed up to her true ability in her classes, and that's our primary motivation for our decision. In fact, if you can, down the line, help us encourage her to work a little harder on her studies, you can be a big help to her. You know, I must say that I'm very impressed with your family. Your mother has done a splendid job with the both of you, you and Ned, and running her business too. And I think she deserves any reward she wants—and I've made it perfectly clear to everybody I know that if she wants membership in the Club, she should have it."

"Thank you very much, Mrs. Martindale. I know she'll be very happy to hear that."

"So, I hope that explains things, a little better, all right? And Marcia asked me, if I talk to you, to give you her love."

"Thank you, Mrs. Martindale. Please tell her I love her too."

"Yes, I know you do. Bye-bye."

April handed the phone back to her mother, and just sat in the kitchen chair, looking down at her hands in her lap. She knew she'd just been told which attitude to take. It was as though all of her spilled feelings had been siphoned up into a tiny tube and made to flow into a little bottle labeled "April," to be placed on some public shelf.

She felt her anger rising again. But she suppressed it. She knew it was hopeless.

And she knew she should be grateful. It was as though Marilyn had said, "I'm taking Marcia away from you, and there's nothing you can do about that. But look! I'm giving you all these nice compliments in return, and a nice gift for your mother and your family." At least that horrible possibility, that Mother's application would be declined, had been dodged.

But the nicest gift Marilyn had given her—as Marilyn might have known full well—was the assurance that Marcia really did love her, and that she hadn't gone away willingly. And that she might see her again. And that would be enough to prevent April from interfering with Marcia's new life. For a while.

"Well? Did we straighten things out?" asked Mother.

176

"Yes," said April. "And Mari . . . Mrs. Martindale said she's backing your application for membership with all her friends."

"Yea!" said Mother. "I gathered she was."

"And she knows my old history teacher, and he told her I was one of his best students."

"Oh, Honey, I'm so proud of you! I really am."

April slept better that night, partly because she was still tired from a couple of nights before. When she got into Ned's car the next morning, she asked if he'd take her with him to the high school instead of to the Club. She wasn't sure what she was doing. She just felt she belonged there, even though it was new to her, and she wanted to sort of confirm, inside herself, that her first summer at the Club was finished.

"Sure," said Ned. "What's up?"

"Oh, I thought I'd try to find Coach Kemp and tell her about Marcia."

"Yeah—Coach Kemp—I think she has an office over by the girls' dressing rooms."

April had to wait for Coach Kemp, but she'd brought along the book she'd been trying for weeks to read. *Call of the Wild.* Robbie had recommended it to her a long time ago. This time she was able to get back into it.

"Well, here's my new star striker," said Coach Kemp, strolling up in shorts and tennis shoes and a khaki shirt, complete with a whistle around her neck. Ready to go. "Good summer? I hear you and Marcia've been swimming over at Brentwood. Caused a little bit of a sensation, from what I hear."

"Well, not hard to do, over there," said April, with a little laugh. Coach Kemp, . . ."

"I've been thinking we're gonna have a pretty strong polo team this year. You know, the way we do it . . . not all the schools in the league can put together a girl's team every year. So we wait, see what we have, and then arrange the meets. There's always a State tournament, but sometimes only three or four schools in the whole state decide to send teams. Anyway, that should improve this year, with Title Nine looming."

"Coach Kemp, Marcia's gone to Palmerston."

"Oh," said Coach Kemp. "Hmm. That's a real loss. Sudden decision?"

"Yes ma'am," said April.

"Oh, well. We lose one or two of those Brentwood girls to Palmerston every year. We always get a team together anyway. You're not going anywhere, are you?"

"Not that I know of," said April. She paused. "The world's full of surprises, isn't it?"

"Yep. You just have to roll with the punches. And if somebody offers you a hand up out of the pool, take it."

After a little conversation with Coach Kemp, about the other girls likely to be on the team and their likely positions—"Of course, we don't know for sure yet"—April walked around and found a bench facing the parking lot, where she'd be sure to see Ned, and settled in to *Call of the Wild.* The only persistent interruption now was a song that kept running through her head. Earlier that morning, she'd realized that she hadn't thought of her song for a while, and had deliberately recalled it. Now she couldn't get rid of it.

> *The Lord is good to me*
> *And so I thank the Lord*
> *For giving me*
> *The things I need . . .*

April was feeling much relieved and relaxed by evening.

"Good workout this morning?" asked Mother. "By yourself, I assume."

"No, I didn't make it this morning. I guess I'll take the week off, rest up a little. I think I need to focus, now, on getting ready for school. Mentally, you know. As well as the other ways."

Mother gave her a curious look. "Yes, well," she said. "Fortunately we already got most of your new clothes together, although you still need to try some of them on." Mother had been doing some more shopping. "Tomorrow we'll need to get your school supplies package, and any other items you may need."

After a while Ned wandered in. They ate leftovers, and April cleared up, as she usually did, this time with Ned's help, as sometimes happened too. They sat and chatted about nothing for a while. Then April stretched, and said she was tired, and went up to bed and resumed the dog book. Within a couple of hours she'd finished it. Robbie was right. It was good. She looked at the author's name. Jack London. She wondered if he'd written any other books.

She turned off the light. For the first time since she'd last seen Marcia, she found she could allow her thoughts to dwell on her. She thought of her bawling at the lake, and of the other times she'd realized that Marcia was crying. She remembered her own feelings of slight surprise and embarrassment at those times, and how those feelings were quickly overtaken by curiosity and sympathy. She didn't recall, at first, that she herself had ever cried while Marcia was with her. It was Marcia's intensity, that only she, April, was allowed to see, that drew her to Marcia, without even knowing she was being drawn. Probably even Dexter never saw it any more, judging from what she said.

April remembered that Marcia had said that April's own intensity—her "fierceness"—was what made her beautiful. She hadn't understood what she meant, but now she did. Marcia's intensity made her beautiful too.

She started thinking about that occasion, their wrestling match, when she'd said that, and when April first experienced Marcia's strength. That's when she remembered that she'd cried along with Marcia. They'd cried together. Then their first daring get-together in the dressing stall. Her astonishment when, covering her eyes with her hands, she first felt Marcia's knuckles rubbing her tummy. She must have jumped a little. April smiled in the darkness, remembering. Marcia muttering something about not

knowing. Leading to Marcia's holding her from behind, her big warm pillow against her shoulder-blades, her hands stroking her tummy and her little puffy breasts.

April noticed she was doing the same thing to herself now. Feeling her chest and her tummy. Feeling them, feeling, softly . . . to try to understand what Marcia felt . . . and to remember . . .

And then, in this very bed, Marcia holding her, so firmly, and squeezing, squeezing, with her hand . . . April suddenly realized that she'd started her dolphin kick—just a little one, but still too much. Too noisy. She stopped immediately, but had to continue squeezing and squeezing . . .

And then her middle fingers slip through her hair, and they start rubbing her clit, which, to her mild surprise, is already swollen. She did that to Marcia. Marcia . . . Marcia getting more and more excited, doing her own little dolphin kick . . .

"Oh Marcia," April whispers again and again. "Oh Marcia."

Printed in Great Britain
by Amazon